Small Town Doctor

Clearwater Novel

Marissa Dobson

Dedication

To Thomas—my wonderful husband.

To all my readers who wanted more Clearwater books, here you go. Thank you for your support.

I hope you enjoy Small Town Doctor as much as I enjoyed getting a change to dive back into the Clearwater town again.

Small Town Doctor

Contents

Small Town Doctor

When pediatrician James Macis rushes to the aid of a woman and her child holed up in a cabin in the mountains just outside of Clearwater, he's uncertain what to think. After spending most of his career in a big city hospital, he's adjusting to the unsteady ways of small town living, but he never expected he'd have to care for a sick child without modern medical supplies.

After some regrettable choices, Ella Carmichael chose to hide, never guessing her decision would jeopardize her daughter's life. Alone in the middle of the woods, she's more terrified than ever. The only thing she wants is for Abbi to be well. For that, she's willing to risk facing civilization again.

James never thought his relocation would give him the chance to have the family he's always wanted. While Ella focused all her efforts on protecting her daughter, the world passed her by. Will a sick child help James and Ella find fulfillment?

Small Town Doctor

Chapter One

The sun was setting over the mountains of Clearwater, Wyoming, bringing another day to a close. Pediatrician James Macis had left a large practice to partner with his brother-in-law, Doctor Michael Johnson. Between the two of them, they were the only pediatricians the tiny town offered. It was a quicker, more routine practice he always thought he wanted, but now that he was here, settling into things, he found that he enjoyed it. He was able to get to know the residents of this small town better than he had ever been able to with any of his clients in Denver.

When he had taken the position, it was to be closer to his sister, nieces, and to give Michael more time with his new family. Now that James was here, he wondered if this wasn't where he always should have been. He fit into Clearwater better than he ever had in Denver. There was no doubt in his mind why Michael loved it here. There was something about a small town that couldn't be found anywhere else, or maybe it was just Clearwater. Everyone acted as if they were part of a family, not just friends or neighbors. People looked out for each other, and when things got tough they stuck together to get through it. James never saw that in Denver.

Another thing Denver didn't offer was the chance to leave the office in the early afternoons for the day. In a small town, his hours decreased, allowing him more time for the activities he enjoyed but never had time for. This past winter, he'd hit the slopes in Jackson Hole more than ever before. During the summer, he swam in the lake, had barbeques, and explored the town. He'd lived in Denver for years, but never saw as much as he had in the last ten months.

Now that fall was upon them and the town was gearing up for Halloween, he was experiencing the joys of the season he'd never known existed before. Next weekend there would be a fair at Clearwater Lake with the main attractions being a pumpkin pie taste test, bake sale, bobbing for apples, and a pumpkin carving competition. It was their last big celebration before Halloween and the iciness of winter. One last chance for the residents to get out and be social before the snow trapped them in their houses. He had to acknowledge he was looking forward to it. The very idea of it put a spring in his step and gave him something to look forward to.

The doorbell forced him to take his gaze off the sky, and he glanced behind him into the house he rented. Without x-ray vision to see who was at the door he was going to have to get up from his relaxing seat on the patio. He grabbed his cell phone off the glass table and started to the door. Crossing the spacious kitchen and living room, he quickly made his way to the front door and pulled it open.

"What can I do for you, Ryan?" He stepped back to let the other man in.

"We need to talk." Sheriff Ryan Ryder walked into the room, his hand on the butt of his gun as though he'd walked right out of a novel about the old west. It was a natural pose for him. His jacket opened enough to reveal the dark blue uniform shirt pulled tight against his broad chest.

"Sure, Sheriff, just come right in." James couldn't keep the sarcasm out of his voice. Since moving here, the two men had become friends but something about this visit said it was business not pleasure that brought him here. "So what can I do for you?"

"Maybe I stopped by to have a beer with you."

James shook his head. "Everything about you screams you're on duty and we both know you don't drink during work hours."

"As sheriff and the only full-time law enforcement, when am I *not* on duty?" Ryan moved farther into the house but didn't take a seat; he stayed standing as though he was on guard.

"When your deputy, Jordan, is on duty, you're not," James reminded him. He'd met Jordan and his wife Chloe two months ago, shortly after she'd given birth to their daughter Bianca. Being a pediatrician, he knew more of the parents and children in town.

"Now that Jordan has finished the house behind Winterbloom Bed and Breakfast, he's able to pick up a few shifts again. Perfect timing with Halloween. Peak season for Jackson Hole is around the corner, which makes our little town busier."

"You didn't stop by to tell me they finished the house? Or that you're going to be busy busting hardened bicycle thieves, so what brings you here?"

With a nod, Ryan adjusted his gun belt. "There's a woman living just outside of town. She's been hiding out there since her daughter was born four years ago."

"Hiding from what?" He wanted to curse himself for his curiosity.

"The child's father brought trouble here a few years ago. He killed a man and got twenty to life in prison. Ella felt she was to blame since she was the reason him and a few of his friends were here. See, she was born and raised in Jackson Hole, the guys were from Cheyenne," Ryan explained. "I arrested him and now I go up every so often to make sure she's okay. I was there today and the little girl needs a doctor."

"What's wrong with her?"

"I don't know the extent of the illness but she's been unable to keep anything down for the last two days. She's burning up with fever, and she's got stomach cramps that have her screaming out in pain."

"She needs to be in the hospital." James couldn't believe his friend who had been a sheriff for years didn't realize how bad the situation was.

"I know she's in bad condition but taking her to the hospital means I have to remove her from her mother's care. She's unwilling to leave the cabin they've holed up in. I've come to you to seek medical care for the child so it doesn't have to come to that."

What Ryan described made it sound like the girl should've been in the hospital, not some backwoods cabin. He didn't have the equipment needed on hand to care for a child that sick, nor did his doctor bag carry fluids the girl so desperately needed.

"Only a hospital has the equipment that will help her," James said, his tone incredulous. "I'm sure she's extremely dehydrated and is in need of fluids. Not to mention tests that should be run to find out the cause of her illness. The flu is bad this year, but what you've mentioned sounds worse than that."

"I understand what I'm asking, but taking Abbi away from her mother isn't going to improve her condition. If anything, it'll make it worse. Abbi has never been around anyone other than her mother. Even after all these years with me visiting occasionally, she hides when I come around. She'll be terrified to be taken away from Ella, especially in a hospital surrounded by all those people. There's a little girl that needs your help, so will you come with me?" When James didn't answer, Ryan added. "You know as well as I do that sometimes in our careers we have to go against the norm for a person's best interests. Bringing medical care to Abbi, instead of taking her to it, *is* in her best interest."

"What if I can't help her?" James asked, doubt creeping in.

"We'll deal with that if it happens." There was a twinge of sadness in Ryan's eyes. "She's pretty bad off and I'm not going to let the girl die. If you say she needs more medical care than you can provide, she'll get it even if it means tearing her away from Ella kicking and screaming."

It was against James's better judgment, but he agreed. "I'll need to stop by my office to get supplies. I'm also going to call Michael."

Ryan's hand rubbed the butt of his gun. "Your brother-in-law has helped on cases similar to this, and I would have gone to him tonight, but with twins I didn't want to risk he might bring some sickness home to them."

James headed away from the entryway to grab supplies he kept on hand when Ryan's words stopped him mid-step. "Cases like this?" Thinking he'd heard the sheriff wrong, he paused and glanced over his shoulder.

"Clearwater is a great small town where most of the locals are average people, but there are others who live in the mountains who are less social. Doctor Bowmen—Richard, the OBGYN—and Michael have gone into the mountains occasionally to assist with difficult births, attend to sick children, whatever is needed." Ryan took his sheriff's hat off and tossed it on the entryway table. "Doc, small town living is different from your big city."

"Don't I know." He moved farther into the house gathering the things he needed, while his thoughts turned back to the office a few days before. After months of being in Clearwater, he hadn't realized a difference until his first barter patient came to his office with his son who'd broken his arm. The man wanted medical care in exchange for a freshly killed deer.

After some negotiation with Michael's help, they agreed Mr. Allen would clean the deer and deliver the meat in exchange for his son's arm being set, placed in a cast, and removed once the time came. If Michael hadn't been in the office, he'd have ended up with a freshly killed deer that still needed to be skinned, cleaned, and cut. It had been an eye opening experience that let him know that he had a lot to learn about his new home. Things were sure different here than in Denver, but he loved living here.

"Come on, James, we really need to go." Panic clung to Ryan's words.

"I'm coming." He grabbed his supplies, then pulled out his cell phone, debating on whether to text or call Michael. He might have some advice on handling situations like this. Instead, he pocketed his cell phone and picked up his pace. He'd deal with Abbi and if he needed advice he'd called Michael then. Right now, Michael had his own family to deal with and since that was his sister and little niece, they mattered a great deal to James as well.

"I'll take my truck and follow you, but remember I need to stop by the office to get more supplies." He grabbed his coat from the banister where he'd tossed it when he came home from the office.

"I can drive us both. It's a rough route to get to their cabin," Ryan warned him.

"You might get a call and have to leave." James shook his head. "I need to have transportation if she declines."

"Without me, you're not going to be able to convince Ella to allow you to take Abbi to the hospital."

"No, *you're* going to make it clear to Ella when we arrive that if the child's health declines *I'll* take her to the hospital with or without her permission. Got it?" He slipped his arms into his jacket. "If you don't make sure Ella understands that, then we're taking her to the hospital now."

"I'll tell her but you're still going to have a fight on your hands." Ryan zippered his coat. "If I have to leave it would be best if you waited until I got back to take her to the hospital."

"That's not always possible." James snatched his keys off the table. "Now let's go."

"Just don't do anything stupid while you're there."

"Never." James followed Ryan out, checking to make sure the door locked behind them. Even though most people in Clearwater didn't lock their doors, he couldn't let go of the habit.

"I've got to pick something up at my place so I'll meet you at your office," Ryan hollered on his way to the police SUV.

"Don't be long, I don't know how to get there."

"I'll be there before you're out." Ryan slid behind the wheel and was gone before James even started his truck.

Maybe it was the big city side of him, but this whole situation made James uncomfortable. If this child was as sick as Ryan described, she needed constant medical care. Care he couldn't provide in a cabin, far from his office, and equipment he might need. But what bothered him the most was Ella was risking her daughter because of guilt. He couldn't understand how a parent could step aside while their child was suffering.

* * *

James carried a bag with electrolyte drinks and bags of fluids for an IV to his truck when he noticed Ryan standing next to it. "I already loaded most of the things, so I think I've got everything." As he went over the list again in his mind, he realized he should have a kit for cases like this in his truck so he'd always be prepared.

"I want you to take this." Ryan held out a gun.

"What would I need that for?" James placed the bag in the back seat of his truck before shutting the door.

"Even though Ella lives out in the middle of nowhere, things can still happen, so if I have to leave you there I want to make sure you're protected."

"That's what you stopped by your place for, isn't it?"

Ryan nodded. "We've gone to Clearwater Combat and Gun shooting, so you know how to use it. Now take it."

"I had Jordan order me a nine millimeter. It's going to be in next week."

"That doesn't help you now. This will." Ryan held the butt of the gun out to him. "Now take it so we can go."

Instead of arguing, he took the gun and hooked the leather holster to his belt. "Let's go, there's a little girl who needs us." He focused on the girl and tried not to think about Ryan's insistence he have a gun. The idea of encountering danger—whether animals or people—in the woods outside of town was a bit overwhelming, especially when he had to care for a sick child in less than ideal conditions.

Small Town Doctor

Chapter Two

Ella Carmichael pressed a cool rag over her daughter's forehead and silently prayed her good health would return. For the first time she questioned her decision to live far away from everyone else. If Abbi's condition worsened before Sheriff Ryder returned, there was nothing she could do. With no means of transport and no phone to call for an ambulance, she couldn't even get Abbi to a hospital.

"Just hang on." It seemed as if the cool rag did nothing to quell raging fever, which only sent another twinge of desperation through her. "My sweet little girl, I'm so sorry. I did this to keep you safe from the worst of my past."

A soft moan escaped Abbi's lips as Ella ran the rag down the child's face, then along her neck. In the four years since Abbi's birth, this was the first time there had ever been a major sickness that terrified her. Up until now, they'd both been reasonably healthy and her daughter had been a happy child.

She straightened when she heard the rumbling of engines approaching along the narrow, overgrown road, and her heart sped up with a mixture of fear and relief. "Ryan's back, sweetie, he's going to make you all better." Abbi didn't open her eyes. "Just hold on, sweetie." Ella tossed the rag into the sink and went to the door to meet them.

The sight of a truck following the sheriff's SUV made her want to bolt the door.

How dare he! She glanced back at Abbi before stepping out of the cabin and shutting the door behind her. With her arms crossed over her chest, she stalked toward Ryan who was exiting his vehicle. "Who the hell is this? You know I don't want anyone here!"

"Ella, I brought Doctor Macis with me. He's a pediatrician in town, so calm yourself or I'll have to detain you."

"*Detain* me? How dare you? We're talking about my daughter here." She charged at Ryan, anger filling her, instinctively lifting her fists.

With one simple sidestep, he pinned her to the side of his SUV, wrapping his hands around her wrists before she could hit him. "This is the only way," he snapped, his voice firm. "Either you stand aside and let him help Abbi or I'm loading her into the SUV and taking her to the hospital myself. Your choice."

She glanced back to the man who had come around the side of the SUV; he didn't look like any doctor she had ever seen with his low-slung jeans and shaggy, curly hair. His casual dress surprised her. The top buttons of his shirt were undone, and she wasn't sure if his easy manner was comforting, unprofessional, or both.

She took him in before turning back to Sheriff Ryder. "You can't do this. Get another doctor from another town…someone who doesn't know."

"Doctor Macis is new to Clearwater, he didn't know what happened. If you don't let him help Abbi I'll make good on my promise."

She shook her head. "No, I can care for her myself."

"Ella, this is your last chance." He used his free hand to reach for his handcuffs. "I'll do it."

Sheriff Ryder's fingers dug into her wrists as the last light peeked through the trees, glimmering on his handcuffs as they came into view.

"Don't make me choose risking my daughter or going to jail," she countered.

"Ma'am, I'm only here to help, please let me see to her." Doctor Macis stepped closer. "While you're wasting time fighting us, your daughter could be getting worse. Now either let us help her or I'll help him detain you. Instead of being there when Abbi wants her mother, you'll be in the back of the SUV waiting to go back to the station. Is that what you want?"

"If you hurt her—"

"I'm only here to help." The doctor held his hands out in front of him as if to say he meant no harm.

"Fine." She tried to shake free from Ryan's grip but he held tight. "Let me go."

"Do I have your word you'll calm down?"

She nodded, and tucked a stray strand of hair behind her ear. "As long as you don't take her from me."

Doctor Macis grabbed the bag he sat on the bumper of the SUV. "Ryan, can you grab the bag from the hood of my truck, while Ms.

Carmichael leads me to the child?" Ryan gave her another look before letting her go and stepping back toward the truck. The doctor moved beside her. "Show me to her and tell me how long she's been ill."

She wanted to scream, to tell him to leave; everything in her wanted this man and everyone else away from her daughter. She knew Ryan, but this stranger set her on edge. Instead, she forced herself to walk toward the house because she didn't want to end up in the Sheriff's handcuffs.

"Abbi's always been healthy, but two days ago she woke up feeling unwell. She so hot and—"

"Ryan mentioned she's been unable to keep anything down. How long has that been going on?"

"Early yesterday." She pushed open the door and was suddenly embarrassed by the small run-down cabin. "I've tried everything to break the fever but—" Her voice cracked.

"I'm going to help her." He stepped past her toward the little girl who lay on a mattress next to the fire.

"I brought her out here by the fire this morning because her skin felt cool to the touch."

"May I?" When she nodded, he went to Abbi and knelt beside the bed, touching her forehead and then her cheek. "Her heartbeat is erratic and she's dehydrated."

"What's wrong with her?" Ella came and squatted down on the other side of the bed.

"I don't know yet, but I'm going to start an IV to give her fluids, that should help her." He hollered over his shoulder. "Ryan, I need that bag."

"Is she going to be all right?" Ella took the little girl's hand in her own.

"I'm going to do everything I can for her."

The way he said that made her stomach sink. Her sweet daughter was in a bad condition, but if she lost Abbi life would no longer have any meaning. The lovely blonde haired, blue-eyed little girl was the only real family she had left. The two of them were alone in the world. Her parents popped into Clearwater occasionally, but things had been strained with them since before Abbi was born. They only came to see their granddaughter, not for Ella.

"Please save my baby." Her voice broke, and tears streamed down her already moistened cheeks.

* * *

Fluids dripped slowly through the IV lines, rehydrating the child while James checked her vitals again. He didn't like how pale and unresponsive she was. She needed to be in a hospital where they could do more for her, but he'd wait a little longer before he forced that. With a miracle they'd see some improvement.

He slipped his stethoscope from around his neck, catching Ryan's attention. "Ella, hold this ice pack to her forehead, I need to get something from my truck." He rose from the bed and moved toward the door knowing Ryan would follow him.

With the cabin door shut behind them, he turned to Ryan. "I've got to get her blood to the lab to see what's wrong with her, but I can't leave her."

"Do you have what you need to draw it?" When James nodded, Ryan continued, "Get it. I'll take it to Michael. He'll rush the order and I'll be back with the results quickly."

"I'll call him and give him the heads-up." James reached into his pocket to pull out his cell phone when Ryan stopped him.

"There's no reception here, even my radio is fading in and out." They walked toward James's truck. "I don't like leaving you out here alone."

"We've got no choice. Just make it clear to Ella that if things start to get worse with Abbi I'm taking her to the hospital." James reached in and grabbed the last bag from the truck, where he kept the tools he needed to take a blood sample. "You're going to need to wait for the results, have Michael look at the report, and send whatever supplies we'll need."

"Fine." Ryan opened the side door to his SUV and reached inside. "The radio is the best communication we have way up here, so keep this. You'll be able to reach me if anything happens. Once the results are back, if you need to bring her to the hospital I'll be able to give you the heads-up. It could scrape a few minutes off the time if I didn't have to come all the way back out here."

"I'm not sure Ella will take it very well if that's the call that needs to be made, but I'll deal with her." James took the radio and glanced back at the house. "I think it's pneumonia but the dehydration and the nasty lung infection is making it appear worse. That little girl is far from out of the woods, she's in a bad condition, but I agree with you. If we're forced to take her to the hospital without Ella it *will* make it worse."

"I'll get back here as quickly as I can." Ryan looked back at the cabin. "Is the girl going to survive?"

"I'm going to do everything I can."

"In other words…you're concerned." Ryan rolled his shoulders before meeting James's gaze.

"Even if she was in the hospital there's no guarantee but I'm not going to give up on her. Let's drawl this blood and get you on your way." Without anything further, he turned and headed back inside the cabin.

He wasn't going to let this girl die on his watch no matter what it cost him. This was outside his comfort zone, but he'd use the same methods. He had the skills to save the girl and now it was time to work the magic.

I didn't work my ass off all those years just to fail now.

He stepped into the cabin and found Ella where he'd left her, huddled next to Abbi. It was clear the fear of losing her only child tightened every muscle in her body—it was the terror of others *and* the girl's sickness. On the trip up the mountain, he couldn't help but question her parenting, why she hadn't been willing to take her to a hospital. Now that he'd met Ella, he could at least see her reasoning, even if he didn't understand it.

Comprehending Ella's reasons was beyond him.

Ella mumbled fairy stories to her daughter, trying to soothe her as she moaned while the fever and pains made her body tremble. It was so different from the life James had growing up. He and his twin sister Jessi were raised by a nanny after their mother died when they were only infants. Their father, a doctor, worked day in and day out until he died of a heart attack at only forty-nine. Four short years ago. Seeing what their father went through was the reason Jessi didn't follow in their footsteps, choosing instead to teach medical classes online. At least before the twins—Kari and Kami—came along. Now she was a full-time mother and wife to Michael. James couldn't help but be envious of the perfect family his sister had, while he was busy working.

He'd be damned if Jessi would ever do this to Kari or Kami. Having a husband and brother who were both pediatricians meant the twins couldn't even sneeze without them both demanding a full work-up.

"Doctor…" Ella called to him, and from the look on her face he could tell she'd said something but he didn't hear her.

"Ella, I apologize. I was thinking. What did you say?"

"Is Abbi going to be okay?"

"I'm doing everything I can for her." He came to kneel next to the bed. "I'm going to do some blood work and Ryan's going to run it down to the lab."

"Why don't you go?" There was a twinge of unease in her voice.

"I need to stay with her and see if we can't get her fever down."

"Ella…" Ryan came closer to the bed than he had the whole time they'd been there. "We need to be clear that if Abbi's condition deteriorates, Doctor Macis is under the authority to take her to the hospital with or without your permission. If you fight him I'll be sure you're arrested for child endangerment, interfering with law enforcement, and anything else I can get to stick. Do you understand me?"

Ella shook her head, sending her blonde hair flying free from a ponytail, her breath coming out in a ragged gasps. She was on the verge of a panic attack.

"Ms. Carmichael, look at me." James waited until she turned her head to face him. "If Abbi's body continues to fail she will go into kidney and possibly heart failure. She will die if we don't get her to the hospital where I can help her more. I know you love your daughter and you don't want that."

"What happens if I don't agree to this?"

"Then the doctor and I will load her into my SUV and take her now." Ryan squatted before her.

"I knew I shouldn't have let you in." A single tear ran down her cheek.

James reached across Abbi and laid his hand over Ella's. "Listen to me. If it comes to taking her to the hospital, it will be her last hope."

"If she leaves here—" She continued to shake her head. "I can't. They hate me for what happened and they'll take it out on my sweet Abbi. The hospital staff won't help her…they will leave her to die. Please, she can't go there."

"Haven't I shown you I'm here to help her?" She nodded in agreement to his question. "I would help her there just as I've done it here. She would be under my care and in good hands, I promise you that."

"I need your word you're not going to fight him if he makes the decision." Ryan stood and adjusted his gun belt.

"If I agree I want you to be the only one who treats her. No one else, I can't risk her."

"I can say I'll do my best, that's all I can promise. Depending on the results of the blood work we might need to bring in a specialized doctor, but I'll oversee everything if that makes you feel better." James squeezed her hand. "Now agree so I can send Ryan with the blood."

"I don't like it but…fine. Just help her." Ella tipped her head to look up at Ryan. "I won't fight him, but if anything happens to her I'll hold you responsible."

"I've been telling you for years that no one blames you and there's no reason for you to stay in hiding." Ryan glanced at Abbi. "It's not good for her. She needs to be around kids her own age. What are you going to do when it's time for her to go to school?"

"This isn't the time for this discussion." James took his hand away from her and unzipped the bag. He needed to get the blood sample taken and send Ryan on his way before he had Ella as worked up as she was when they arrived. She had just calmed to his presence and he didn't want her in a nervous state again.

"Ella, could you grab more ice packs from that bag." He nodded to the one sitting on the edge of the sofa. "The fluids are helping to bring more color to her cheeks but the fever isn't breaking. In another thirty minutes we can give her another dose of the medication I brought." He tied off her arm, finding the best vein he could in order to get the blood he needed.

"What happens if it doesn't break the fever?" She grabbed two of the ice packs.

"Bend them, it will crack them, and become instantly cool." He nodded to the ice packs. "As for the fever, Ryan's going to pick up another medication while he's in town." If the fever didn't subside by morning, the hospital would be the only option. He wouldn't risk long-term brain damage because of Ella's irrational fears. "Don't worry, Ella, we're going to make sure she's okay." Even after all these years as a pediatrician, a sick child still tore at his heart.

Small Town Doctor

Chapter Three

The sun had set long ago when Ella stepped outside into the cool night air. Only a few stars spotted through the sky, shinning like diamonds in the darkness. The moon played peak-a-boo with the clouds, so every once in a while a glimpse of it could be seen through the trees. Being out in the middle of the woods, surrounded by only the trees and wild animals had always been peaceful for her. Now that her daughter lying unconscious just inside the cabin, she was restless and doubting her decisions of the last few years.

She took a deep breath of the fresh air she needed so badly to clear her thoughts, letting the cool night air fill her lungs until it chilled her from the inside out. Exhaustion ate at every muscle in her body and closing her eyes made her feel as if she was rubbing them along a line of sandpaper. For two days, she'd avoided sleep, scared of what would happen to Abbi if she wasn't awake to keep watch. Now her body was revolting, demanding rest before she passed out. Logical thoughts were almost beyond her, as her brain jumped from one thing to the next without any rhyme or reason.

Had she made the wrong decision when she moved to her grandparent's old cabin, away from civilization and the mistakes she'd made? Worse yet, would that decision cause her to lose her daughter? Her legs gave out from under her and her fears pressed down on her shoulders until she collapsed on all fours.

"Please let him save my baby girl." She cried out but no one heard her.

Doctor Macis was inside with Abbi, still waiting for word from the sheriff on the results of the blood work.

Every minute that passed when there were no wheels crunching the debris on the overgrown road and no communication on the radio, only served to worry her more. Where was Ryan? Why had he not returned with the supplies the doctor needed and news on what was wrong with her daughter?

"Ms. Carmichael." The doctor stepped up behind her, and she realized she was still on the ground. "Are you all right? What happened?"

The concern in his voice for her and her daughter was the only reason she'd trusted him so far. She could tell he was a good doctor. As they waited, he held the same anxiety she did, while they both checked the clock and glancing to the radio Ryan left.

"I'm fi…fine." Her voice cracked before she forced herself to swallow.

"What are you doing on the ground? You're going to end up sick and we can't have that." He wrapped his arm around her shoulders. "Come on, let's get you back inside."

"My baby…" Tears welled in her eyes. "I did this to my sweet Abbi and now she's dying because of me."

He squeezed her tighter to him. "We're not going to let that happen."

Unable to hold back the tears any longer, she let her head fall against his shoulder. "I'm an awful parent."

He pulled her up until they were both standing in a ray of moonlight, his hands on her shoulders as he stood in front of her. "I might not know the full story but I can see you're not a bad parent. You care for your daughter."

"If I'm such a good mother, she'd be in the hospital. You said so much yourself when you arrived. What kind of parent lets their child suffer like this?"

"One who lets fear control her actions." She started to pull away from him but he held tight. "No, I'm not going to let you pull away out of fear or anger, not this time. Ella, you're scared, and I understand that but we're going to make sure Abbi is okay. We've broke her fever and that's one step in the right direction."

"My Abbi." She used the back of her hand to wipe the tears away from cheeks.

"You're scared because of what you've been through, so you stay hidden away from everyone…but that isn't good for either of you. This isn't just about the medical care. There are other negative aspects to you living up here. Abbi needs kids her own age to play with."

"Doctor Macis, I'm not neglecting my daughter."

"Call me James, please…and not in every way." He ran his hand down her arm. "You care for Abbi's needs. You keep her healthy, active, and the books in her room show you've started her education.

I'm only offering my suggestion that you need to balance the life you want and socialize her. You know as much as I do that she needs other children to play with. There's no reason you can't go into town occasionally and give her that."

"There's every reason. Did Ryan tell you why I chose to live here?"

"No." He tipped his head back to the cabin. "If you want to tell me, let's go inside. You're already worn down from caring for Abbi, you don't need to be out here in the cold evening air."

The breeze whipped her hair as she let him lead her back into the cabin. She glanced back out at the woods but no longer found security or safety in the darkness of the trees. Or maybe she was letting her fears carry her way.

"Why don't you pour us coffee and I'll check on Abbi." He stalked off to Abbi's bedroom, where they'd moved her once her fever broke so she was resting comfortably in her bed again.

"Is she okay?" She called to him, but he'd already disappeared around the corner. Instead of following him, she moved to the small kitchen and grabbed the metal coffee pot from the wood burning stove.

She was sure her humble little cabin was nothing to the doctor, especially since she remembered Ryan mentioning he'd come to Clearwater from Denver. Nevertheless, the cabin was home to her. There wasn't electricity, but she managed with solar power for the few lights they had. The fireplace heated the small abode and the wood burning stove served her fine. The well and septic gave them all the amenities needed and they didn't have to rough it by fetching water from the nearby creek or using an outhouse like her grandparents had years ago.

She'd turned the small cabin into a home for her and Abbi. The only thing missing was children for Abbi to play with. That was one thing that no matter how much Ella wanted she couldn't give her that. It meant they'd have to go into town and she couldn't get past her fears.

"You're a million miles away."

She turned to find James standing behind her and she almost dropped the pot of coffee. "I was thinking."

"Care to share?"

She filled two mugs before turning back to him. "You're right, Doctor Macis. I've known for a while now that Abbi needs playmates, friends, but I can't help that."

"What do I have to do for you to call me James?" He smirked at her before taking the mug of coffee from her.

"Sorry, it's been so long since I've had to deal with anyone...." She paused, uncertain. "James, what am I supposed to do? I can't give her what she needs."

"We'll take care of it. First we need to make sure she's well again." He laid his hand on her arm. "Tell me why you're so scared. What did the town's residents do that made you sneak away to the mountains?"

"Not what they've done, more like what *I've* done." She slipped out of his grasp and moved across the open space to the sofa by the fireplace. "I brought danger and death to Clearwater."

He came and sat down on the sofa, keeping his distance from her. "How?"

She raised an eyebrow in question. Did he really not know what happened or was he just digging for more gossip? "Are you telling me Ryan told you *nothing* about why we we're living so far up the mountain?"

"He mentioned very little." He sat the mug on the coffee table before them. "I'd like to know what actually happened but I won't pressure you. If you wish to tell me then it will be your decision. Otherwise I'll see if I can get Ryan on the radio."

"You were trying that before I went outside with no luck." She took a sip of coffee. "After my grandparents passed away my parents moved back to Dad's hometown, Cheyenne. I was visiting them when I met Josh, Abbi's father. A few months after my trip down there Josh and a few of his buddies came to visit. It was when I was living in Jackson Hole."

"I get the impression something went wrong on that visit."

"*Everything* that could possibly go wrong went wrong. The whole trip was a disaster." She set the mug aside. "Josh and his friends went wild. They were drinking, doing drugs, and as the days went by things became worse. Until the visit ended in senseless bloodshed."

"What happened?"

"Josh decided we had to go to the bar in Clearwater, On the Rocks. Knowing he'd drink until he could barely walk, I wanted to stay in Jackson Hole." She closed her eyes as memories of that night came flooding back. It was the first time Josh had become violent, but it hadn't been the last. It was only a sample of what was coming after they left the bar. "That's when things got out of hand."

"Ryan mentioned he killed a man. Is that where it happened?"

"Yes. He got into it with a guy at the bar. Instead of keeping Josh in check, his friends took off, leaving me trying to stop him, but I couldn't. H...he flung me aside and...I banged my head on the corner of the bar. I must have passed out because when I came to everyone was in the parking lot and Josh...he was beating the guy's head into the sidewalk." She wrapped her arms around her waist, hugging herself. "I screamed for him to stop and when he looked up...it was like he was a different person. The eyes that stared back at me were not his. I didn't know who was in front of me and it scared me."

"It's okay." He scooted across the sofa, coming closer to her, and wrapped his arm around her shoulders. "He can't hurt you or anyone else any longer."

"Not now but he left plenty of scars on me as a lasting memory."

"This is why you've taken refuge here?" He caressed her shoulder, offering welcome comfort.

"Ryan believes I did it because I'm afraid of what the town residents think of me. Maybe that's part of it...but there's something more terrifying." She wanted to curl into his embrace, to wrap herself in the first comforting touch she'd felt in years.

"Tell me why."

"Josh is Abbi's father. I...I've seen the worst in him and I'm terrified it's part of my baby girl. I must stay here to keep her away from others. I'm scared of what her temper will be like if she's faced with ridicule, or learns what her father did. This is the only way."

"Ella, look at me." He used his forefinger to guide her chin until she looked up at him. "It's more about how the child is raised than genetics. A child mimics actions they see from others. If he was here with you, it's likely she could see his anger, how he uses it to control you or others, and she might do the same. That isn't the case."

"How do you know?"

"Ryan speaks highly of you and how you're raising Abbi. His only concern is she's not being socialized, and that's my concern as well." He used the back of his hand to wipe away the stray tear that was rolling down her cheek. "The love you show her every day is going to ensure she's raised right."

She shook her head. "You don't know that."

"I'm a doctor. I've seen and worked with children with temper issues. Not once in all the time I've been here have you or Ryan gave me any reason to be concerned about Abbi. There's also something else you need to consider…everyone has a temper but that doesn't mean they'll kill someone. Some people have tempers that are easier to spark than others, but there are also other outlets for the anger. You can teach Abbi ways to control her rage. If it would make you feel better I can speak with her once she's feeling better, to evaluate her."

"No, she must not know what Josh did."

"I wouldn't tell her anything of the kind. You can be there when I speak with her if you'd like. I'm offering to give you some peace of mind, not because I believe she'll say anything that makes me concerned." He let his hand fall away from her cheek. "I think it would help you if you get the rest of the story about Josh off your chest. Ryan mentioned he arrested Josh…did he show up at the bar?"

"No." She pulled away, just enough that his arm was still around her but enough to give her some space. "Josh forced me back into his truck. We couldn't go back to my apartment because he thought the police would be waiting for us. My grandfather had another cabin about halfway down the mountain. It's where he lived before he build this place and married my grandmother. We went there, but it's closer to the main road. One of the residents saw Josh's truck and Ryan showed up."

"Alone?"

"Sheriff Ryder is a one man team…or haven't you heard that yet?" She tried to make light of it.

"Oh, I've heard." He leaned back against the sofa. "He hired a deputy, part-time, but he's always on call, never takes a day off."

"When Ryan showed up things were heated, or maybe a better word is *bloody*. Josh thought while I was in the bar I had called the police and he…he nearly killed me for it." She swallowed deep before continuing. "Ryan busted down the door and pulled Josh off me. He got a few extra punches in my honor before he handcuffed him. That was the last time I saw him. Thankfully, they didn't need me to testify at his trial, so I didn't even go. He doesn't even know he's a father."

"If I can convince you that you have nothing to worry about with Abbi's temper, will you bring her into town occasionally to socialize her?" He leaned forward to look at her.

"I don't know." She glanced toward Abbi's bedroom before looking back at him. "I just don't know. I want her have friends her own age, but what if they tell her what Josh did?"

"You can't protect her forever, but if there's one thing I know about Clearwater…it's the best place to live. The residents want to put what happened behind them as much as you do. They don't want their children to know about what happened. Clearwater residents shelter their children from what other areas have to deal with. I don't believe anyone will mention what happened to Abbi, nor do I think anyone holds what happened against you. From what you told me they saw Josh attack you just as he attacked others."

She was questioning if he was right when a scream cut through her heart. "Mommy!"

"I'm coming." She rushed to her daughter's bedroom as fear gripped her. To hear Abbi call for her after being unconscious for so long both excited and terrified her. They'd broken the fever hours ago but this was the first sign of recovery Abbi had shown. What else would they face before her daughter was the same cheerful little girl she'd been only days before?

Chapter Four

James was nearly on Ella's heels as they raced toward Abbi's room. The cry might have been enough to start Ella dashing to the child's bedroom but it was the coughing fit that sped his pulse. He suspected it might have been pneumonia or at the very least a nasty lung infection, but now that she was awake he was seeing evidence of the cough.

"Mommy." The little girl cried out as Ella came through the entryway.

"It's all right, sweetie. Mommy is right here."

At the bedside, James stood just behind Ella. "I need to check her vitals."

"Sweetie, this is Doctor Macis, he came to help you feel better." She moved back, giving him access to Ella.

"Abbi, I'm just going to listen to your lungs, okay?" He moved the girl's shirt aside to press his stethoscope to her chest. He had just started to listen to what he needed to hear when Ella interrupted him.

"Listen."

"That's what I was trying to do." He glanced up to see she was looking toward the doorway. He quickly pulled the stethoscope from his ears when he heard the sheriff's radio that he left next to the sofa crackle to life. "I got it. Stay with her and don't let her get out of this bed. She needs to rest." He shot off the mattress and nearly ran back to the living room. Hopefully this was good news. He'd made progress with Ella but he didn't think she was ready to be thrown into the Clearwater social scene…and that would most certainly happen if they had to take Abbi to the hospital.

"James, come in, James." The radio crackled to life, filling the small space with Ryan's voice.

He snatched the radio off the coffee table and brought it closer to his mouth. "I'm here. What the hell has taken you so long?"

"There was a car accident at Main Street and Crawford Lane. A visitor to Winterbloom took the curve too quickly and nearly ended up part of the church." The static had Ryan's voice fading in and out.

"What news do you have for me about Abbi?"

"Results are back. It's pneumonia. There were a few other questions raised about the blood work, but Michael's on his way up. I'm still at the scene dealing with the clean-up, but Michael knows the way, he was there after Abbi was born. He'll honk his horn when he arrives, meet him outside."

"Got it. He better be bringing supplies."

"He is and I'll be up once I get this mess cleared up. Any change with the child?" In the background there was a man hollering at someone but James couldn't make out the words.

"We broke her fever and she's awake."

"Good. I'll be there when I can." Ryan ended the conversation and was back to work as the town's Sheriff.

James stood there for a moment, radio in hand, his thoughts scattered. The knowledge Abbi had pneumonia and not something worse made the muscles in his shoulders relax a bit.

"Is Ryan on his way back?"

He turned to find Ella in the doorway, her arms crossed over her midriff. "No, my brother-in-law is going to bring medication that should help her."

"Brother-in-law?"

He could see the fear rising in her eyes. He wanted to go to her, wrap his arms around her. Everything in him wanted to tell Ella he'd protect her, but he barely knew the woman and couldn't go making promises he couldn't keep. She deserved better than that and didn't need her first encounter with people, after so much isolation, to be one that was uncomfortable. He took a step forward before stopping himself. "Doctor Michael Johnson. Ryan said he's been here before."

She nodded, but the fear didn't leave her eyes. "He was here after I gave birth to Abbi."

"There's no need to worry, he's only bringing the medication I need. Abbi has pneumonia, she needs things I don't have with me." He crossed the space until he was standing just in front of her. "He's not coming in, so you don't have to worry. My sister Jessi is his wife, and they have twin girls, Kari and Kami. I don't want him taking the germs to the girls. You don't have to worry about anything. You can wait in here with Abbi while I get the supplies and he'll be on his way. No harm done."

"He was a good doctor, but he'd have pushed for Abbi to go to the hospital. He didn't agree with me raising her out here."

"If anyone would have understood I thought it would be Michael. He was born here, only leaving while he was in medical school." He touched her arm. "It doesn't matter because she's staying right here for now anyway."

"So she doesn't have to go to the hospital?"

He shook his head. "As long as she continues to improve." Even as he said it, he knew there was a major catch in that.

"Oh, thank you." She wrapped her arms around his neck, hugging him. "Thank you for saving my baby."

"She's not out of the woods yet. Her lungs still sound congested and it's likely she has a lung infection too." She let go of him and stepped back. "Now that we've got her rehydrated, I'm going to start her on a different IV once Michael arrives and that will speed her recovery. However, you're going to have to make a decision, though I suspect I know your answer."

"What would that be?" She leaned back against the wall.

"You have no phone, no transportation, and no options if something changes. I can't leave her here when there's no way for you to get help."

"Wait, you just said—"

"Let me finish." He shoved his hands into the pockets of his jeans. "Either she comes down to the hospital, and I'll make sure you have a private room, with no one else caring for besides me, or…"

"Or?" She looked at him when he paused.

"Or I'll have to stay here."

"You'll what?" She stepped away from the wall, her eyes wide with shock.

"It's the only way. If I'm here I can help her, and if for some reason her condition worsens, we can take her into town. So…do I get to bunk on your sofa tonight, or shall I begin loading my truck?" He turned as if to start gathering the supplies he'd laid out on the coffee table.

She grabbed hold of his arm before he could step away from her. "You can have the bed in my room and I'll sleep with Abbi."

"You'd get more sleep in your room, and I'll need to check on Abbi occasionally throughout the night."

"I'd rather stay with her to ensure she's fine." She glanced to the window. "I haven't had much of an appetite myself but I'm sure you're hungry. I'll whip you up something to eat while you finish checking Abbi's vitals."

"I appreciate it, but I just need more coffee."

"Coffee? I thought it was a myth that doctors lived on that." The humor in her eyes wasn't there long. "Pneumonia…that's how my grandmother died."

"It's not like that. Pneumonia is deadly to those who are already ill, the very young and the old. Abbi's young, but besides, you said she's been healthy. We're going to make sure she's fine, now don't you worry."

He'd be damned if he'd let Abbi die. In the last few hours the little family had stolen his heart. Now he knew why Ryan was willing to go out of his way to help them, to go against the grain just to get the little girl medical care without disrupting the family dynamics. He was willing to do the same. Did he still think Abbi could be helped more in a hospital than in the cabin? Yes, but it wasn't that simple any longer. It was more about what was in the best interest of the child, and the best thing for her was to keep her home. For the first time in his life he understood why some people chose to remain at home when they were sick or dying.

This little trip into the mountains of Clearwater gave him a new perspective in his medical training. He actually understood what the family went through. He wasn't a good doctor just because of the training but because he was compassionate and could understand them, what they needed. But he'd never been in a situation like this before.

He was going to make sure little Abbi made a perfect recovery, and then he was going to work on getting Ella to trust him. To trust the residents of Clearwater. She could choose to live in the mountains, but both her and Abbi needed socialization.

I'm going to make you trust me, Ella Carmichael. No matter what.

He wondered about his motives, his emotions. Something about Ella tugged at his heart, but he couldn't pinpoint it. He'd find out what it was—soon. In the meantime, Abbi needed him.

* * *

Almost an hour after the radio crackled to life, the sound of tires crunching up the roadway brought James to his feet. He crossed the living room and had his hand on the door before the truck stopped. He wanted to get Michael on his way as quickly as he could to ease Ella's worries.

"I'll be back in a minute," he called over his shoulder as he opened the door.

The cool night air made him wish he'd grabbed his jacket before stepping outside. There had to be a fifteen degree difference between Clearwater and these mountains. Even in October with the fall leaves scattering the ground he could feel the chill of winter in the air, threatening to wrap its tentacles around the sleepy little town and hold on tight until long after the New Year.

"How's your first call into the wild going?" Michael smirked as he stepped from his truck.

"A different experience all together but I'm rolling with the punches. How's my sister and the twins?"

"The girls are asleep and Jessi is going over Halloween decorations with our housekeeper, Cathy. She wants it to be perfect for the Halloween party. You'll be there, won't you?"

James nodded and came to stand next to the truck, a thought stirring in the back of his mind. "I might bring someone if that's okay."

"Anyone I know?" Michael leaned against the door, grinning. "Jes will be so happy you're seeing someone."

"Not actually seeing someone. I'd like to bring Ella and Abbi—"

Michael's eyes widened. "You what? You're barking up the wrong tree. She's a recluse and she's never coming off this mountain."

"She's scared."

"So, now she's your charity case?" Michael crossed his arms over his chest and watched him.

"No, nothing like that." James glanced back to the house, hoping Ella hadn't heard what Michael said. He didn't want her to get the wrong idea, just when he'd started to make some progress. "I don't think she wants to be locked up here, away from everyone, but she's scared. She's a sweet woman who deserves a chance at life. She was frightened when she took off and came up here, now she feels like she doesn't have a choice. I can show her the residents don't blame her."

"She hasn't trusted anyone in years. If you hurt her in any way, it's going to make it harder for her to trust anyone else." Michael glanced toward the house. "If you screw this up you might be the reason she stays locked up in this cabin for years to come. Are you really willing to risk that?"

"I'm not going to hurt her." He'd go out of his way to make sure she wasn't hurt by anyone. All he wanted to do was protect her. To see her happy and living a normal life. "I understand it's a gamble but it's the only way. For years Ryan tried to get her to come back into town without making any progress, but just in a few hours I've been able to get her to see reason. To see what being a recluse is doing to her daughter. Abbi needs children her own age to play with, interactions with other adults. It isn't about living in a cabin in the woods. She could still do that, I just want her to see she needs more than this."

"You better know what you're doing."

"I think I do." James reached into the back seat of the truck. "Now tell me about this blood work so you can get back to your family."

"The white blood cells were extremely high, as you'd expect. However, it tells us the girl is extremely anemic. It's low enough that I recommend bagged iron transfusions to bring it up. Then a daily iron pill, possibly for life, but at least for the next six months."

"At her age I wouldn't do the transfusion here, it's too far from the hospital if she has an adverse reaction."

Michael nodded and handed the paperwork to James. "Being that it's the weekend I thought you could use the office. That's if you can get her agree to it. No one will be there and you're close enough that if anything happens you only have to go out to the main hall and up a few floors to the children's ward."

James scanned the printouts. "No wonder Abbi's been so tired lately, and she's been suffering with this for some time. I'll convince Ella this is needed, otherwise it will be hard for the child to recover from pneumonia."

"If you convince her, give me a call I'll come to the office if you need assistance."

"Thanks." He grabbed the last of the supplies from the truck and shut the door. "I'll let you know and I do appreciate you bringing this stuff up."

Michael paused. "James, you'd better know what you're doing. You could end up doing more harm than good."

"I know the risks, but they *are* worth it."

Michael got into the truck, starting the engine, and rolled down the window. "You better be ready for whatever this brings. Even if that means next time Ryan has to remove the girl from her custody because she won't allow either of us here."

James stepped out of the way as Michael turned around and drove back down the mountain. He tried to push the doubts from his mind. The idea he could hurt Ella and Abbi when all he wanted to do was help them made his stomach roil. If he could wrap them up and keep them safe from everything and everyone that could harm them, he would.

Wait, that's just what I'm trying to keep them from. Ella needs to see there's so much more to life. He tried to tell himself he wanted nothing more…but that was a lie, and even his subconscious knew better.

Chapter Five

The truck pulled away from the house and Ella's temper rocketed through the roof. How dare he think of them as a charity case? She didn't need anyone's charity; she'd chosen this life. Damn him for making her think he was any different. For being a man she thought she could trust, then turning out to be just another asshole. It was one thing for someone to let her down—she had been dealing with it most of her life—but she'd be damned if Abbi was hurt. Her daughter was her life, her reason for living, and she didn't want her to have to deal with the same things she had.

The last time she spoke to her parents they'd begged her to come to Cheyenne, to make a life there so they could be close to Abbi and then Ella could begin to date again, to make a proper family for the little girl. What her mother didn't seem to understand is she didn't want a string of men coming in and out of Abbi's life. Dating with a small child, not to mention the past they had, was difficult if not nearly impossible. A lot of men ran at the idea of having a step-child. She wouldn't put her daughter through that, no matter how much she might miss the company of a man. The company of others in general.

The front door creaked open and James stepped inside. The sight of him had her moving away from the kitchen window, rage coursing through her body. She wanted to scream and fight, to force him to leave, but that would only hurt her daughter. Abbi was still sick and she needed the antibiotics that had just been delivered. To force him to leave could make Abbi sick again, or worse, the decision could mean Ryan would try to take her away. No, she'd wait until her daughter was healthy and then she'd make him go away.

"I've got what we need but there was a little more information in the blood work." He placed what he'd carried in on the coffee table. "I'm going to get these antibiotics started."

"Fine." She held onto the counter, pushing the edge into her hand to ground her and keep her from hitting him.

"Is something wrong?" He watched her for a moment.

"It's fine, just go about your business. I have things I must attend to." She forced herself away from the counter and out the kitchen door to where she kept the wood stacked for the fireplace. There was no need for more wood yet, but she needed something to busy herself with. Fetching wood was a mundane task and didn't require her to stay focused on it. She could let her mind work through the rage that boiled within her.

She tipped her head back, the wind whipping her hair around her face, and tried to let the coolness chill her temper. She couldn't understand why she was so worked up about this, why she'd let a man she barely knew get under her skin. He wasn't the first one who disappointed her, and if she left this cabin he wouldn't be the last. She wasn't sure how long she stood there but a throat clearing behind her pulled her back to reality.

"Ella."

"Is something wrong with Abbi?"

He came to stand next to her. "I started the antibiotic and for now she's resting comfortably. Michael brought the blood work results with him and it turns out Abbi is anemic. She needs to have a bagged iron transfusion but I can't do that here, we'll need to take her into town. Tomorrow."

"No."

"No?" He stepped around to stand in front of her. "What do you mean no? Do you understand what it means for her health? Or the fact this has been an ongoing issue and now it's bad enough that it's showing in her behavior? It's the reason she's been so tired lately, why she has those dark circles under her eyes, and why she's so pale."

"We're talking about my daughter and she's staying here. I don't need or want your charity!"

"What are you talking about?"

The fact he had to ask sparked the return of her anger. Without thinking she brought her arm up and smacked him across the face. The palm of her hand stung, and his cheek reddened. "How dare you deny it! I could hear you through the window with Michael."

He took a step back, out of her striking zone. "You heard my brother-in-law being an ass, nothing more. He doesn't know what he's talking about."

"Well, I won't be considered a charity case for anyone. I don't need it or want it." She raised her voice several notches.

"That's not why I'm here, or why I care." He shoved his hands into the front pockets of his jeans. "I want to help you, is that so wrong?"

"You want to help because you feel sorry for us. Well there's no reason to. I chose this."

"I know the decisions you made, you've made it clear to me multiple times since I've been here. That isn't the reason I want to help you."

"Then why are you doing it?" She met his gaze.

"You've been wronged in the past, I suspect by more than just Josh, but not everyone is like that. I'm not like that. You need to trust someone and I'm asking that you trust me." He took a step closer to her. "I'm not doing this because I feel bad for you. Actually, I think you have it pretty well here. You live life on your terms not someone else's. Yes, I would like to see you and Abbi more socialized, for her to have children her own age to play with. Though there are plenty of children who are homeschooled and don't have many interactions with others, and they grow up to be fine adults. Ella, I want you to trust me, let me show you Clearwater is a safe place for you and your daughter."

"Why should I trust you?"

"I think the better question is why shouldn't you? I know you've been hurt in the past but you have to start somewhere. I'm a safe place to start. Haven't I kept my word so far? I haven't pressed for Abbi to go to the hospital. I'm doing what I can for her here."

"Then why can't you do this transfusion here?"

"Most people have no adverse reactions to the iron supplements but it's possible. We don't do bagged iron often, it's used only when it's imperative that the iron levels start to recover quickly. I feel Abbi needs this or I wouldn't recommend it. It's the weekend so my office is closed. It's attached to the back of the hospital, connected through a staff-only entrance. We could go there for the treatment. That way we're close to what I'll need if anything should happen."

"What do you mean *if anything happens?* What are the chances?" She ran her hand down her arm, chasing a chill away.

"It's slim but we must take precautions. She'd be able to tell us if anything is wrong and we can take the countermeasures. I wouldn't recommend this if I didn't it was safe. A transfusion will help her to start to feel better, she won't be as tired, and the iron supplement she can take daily will continue to assist her." He came to stand in front of her and placed his hand on her arm, gently rubbing it. "I wouldn't do anything to risk her."

"What happens if I don't agree?"

"The transfusion is something I can recommend but cannot push. Abbi is a minor, you're the one who has to make the decision. Even adults have to sign off on the transfusion because the government recommends iron be delivered in smaller doses. Even Ryan couldn't force you to do this and I'm not going to mention it to him." He caressed along her shoulder and down the length of her arm. "I want this to be your decision and if you're more comfortable doing the pill supplements we can try that. The transfusion is a quicker way to start so she would start to see results right away."

"I need time to think about it."

"That's fine. We can use my office anytime throughout the weekend or evenings. Now let's go inside."

She let him lead her in and toward the warmth of the fireplace. "It's crazy, but I do trust you…so when I heard Michael saying you were only here because of charity it upset me. I figured you weren't the first person to fail me but I wouldn't let it happen to Abbi."

"I'm not going to hurt you or Abbi. You have to trust someone, so why not me? If you let me, I'll take you into town and prove to you that you have nothing to be concerned about."

"One step at a time. Right now Abbi's health is the most important thing." She sat down on the sofa. "You know so much about me but I barely know you. Tell me about yourself. Where are you from? What made you become a doctor?"

"My sister, Jessi, and I are from outside of Denver. Our mother died when we were infants, leaving us to be raised by a nanny while our father who was a doctor worked long hours. He died of a heart attack a few years ago, at forty-nine." He sat down next to her and leaned forward until his elbows were on his knees. "I became a doctor because it was what was expected. My father wanted both of us to, but Jessi chose teaching. I wanted to please my father but not follow in his footsteps. He was a surgeon."

"So why did you become a pediatrician?"

"It's not a very original idea but I wanted to work with children. Seeing them come into the office happy and healthy brings joy to my day and when they are sick it breaks my heart but I know my skills can make them feel better."

"I understand. Before everything happened I was taking college classes. I wanted to be a teacher to work with special education students. Then everything changed."

He turned enough to lay a hand on her leg. "It's not too late."

"I think it is. No one would want me teaching their children." One stupid decision made and she'd forever have to suffer with it.

"I'm going to prove you wrong. I'm going to take you into town and you're going to see that no one holds you responsible."

She wanted him to be able to prove her wrong more than anything in the world. To be able to have more of a life than what she had would be wonderful, but fear held her back. Years ago she had been full of life, never letting fear or anything else hold her back from what she wanted. Now she was too frightened to leave the confines of the cabin because of someone else's actions. *What happened to me? Why did I let Josh break my spirit? Even though he's not here…he still controls my actions.*

* * *

It was the first night Abbi hadn't been deathly sick and it should have been time for Ella to catch up on sleep. Instead, she lay in bed staring at the ceiling. Her thoughts on what to do were jumbled—everything from the iron transfusion to how to handle things with James. She wanted to trust him but was worried she was misreading things. Was he doing this to be friendly, or for more personal reasons?

She had little experience with men and the most recent one was Josh, which wasn't anything to go by. James was an attractive man and she was sure he could have any woman he wanted. So why did she think he was attracted to her? Maybe it was the way she caught him looking at her when he didn't think she was watching. Or the way he had caressed her shoulder earlier.

It was possible she was misreading it, needing or wanting more attention than she was actually getting. Damn, she hoped she wasn't misjudging the situation. She wanted to feel his arms around her. She was so lonely, so full of desire. He wasn't a man who would live here with her; he needed to be in town, close to his friends and family, but he could take the edge off her hunger for sure.

It had been over four years since she'd felt the touch of a man. *Too damn long.* To feel the gentle caresses would rejuvenate her enough to continue making the best life possible for Abbi. She always thought she'd only wanted to be touched by someone who loved her, now she realized love was overrated. Love meant she'd get hurt in the end. She thought Josh loved her, but he only used her.

No, I'm done with love.

Chapter Six

James stood by the counter trying to wake up after a night of tossing and turning, as he waited for the coffee to finish percolating. He had slept in Ella's bed surrounded by her scent, mixed with the sweet strawberry from her shampoo, sending his thoughts of her swirling out of control. The last thing she needed was him thinking about getting her naked. The most important thing was getting her to trust him. Trust was a big thing in all relationships, but it would be even more important with Ella. She was already looking for a reason to shut him out, to use it as an excuse to protect her heart.

He took a deep breath, breathing in the rich aroma of the coffee, and used that moment of alertness to remind himself why he was here. He wasn't here to seduce Ella, but to be a doctor for Abbi. Long ago from his father's actions he learned not to date someone he worked with, but it was the same with dating a parent of a patient.

"Morning."

He turned to find Ella standing in the doorway of Abbi's room, her gray yoga pants clinging to the curve of her hips, and the white tank top barely reaching her waist, giving a glimpse of her stomach when she moved a certain way. Her hair lightly tousled from sleep made him want to draw his fingers through it. He wanted to go to her and wrap her in his arms. Instead, he forced himself to stay where he was.

"Coffee is almost done."

"Sorry, I should have been up earlier." She dragged her hands through her hair, pulling the long strands away from her face.

"You've been caring for a sick child for the last few days, it's understandable you'd be tired. Why don't you sit down and I'll bring you a cup when it's finished."

"I should make breakfast."

He grabbed two mugs from the rack. "Let's talk first. Have you had a chance to think about the transfusion?"

"All night."

"What have you decided?" He poured the coffee, before going to where she stood by the sofa.

She took hold of the coffee he offered but didn't take a drink of it. "After you checked on her at four this morning she had a hard time going back to sleep so we laid there talking, telling stories. She seems so much better."

"The antibiotics and fluids have done a lot to help her, but don't let that fool you. She's still sick and needs to take it easy for a few days." He sat down next to her on the sofa. "The round of powerful antibiotics finished throughout the night so I can remove her IV line when she wakes up and she can move around the house easier. If we're not going to do the transfusion then I'll need to make a trip into town for the iron pills and some additional antibiotics."

"What's the worst that will happen if I decided not to do it? Will it kill her?"

He set the coffee aside and took her hand into his. "No. She'll be tired and require more sleep. She might be more irritable, have occasional headaches, and if it gets worse she could have shortness of breath and trouble concentrating. Though I don't think we have to worry about that for now, her levels are low but not dangerously low where we need to be overly concerned."

"Is there anything I can do besides the treatment that will help her?"

"There's an iron supplement I'll pick up in town that she can take twice a day. Eating more iron rich food would be beneficial as well, and I'll get you a list of those too. Should I take it you've decided against it?"

She set the coffee down and turned to him. "Yes, but not because of going into town. You mentioned the risks of the treatment and I'm concerned about that, especially with her current health. I want to wait and see if the pills will be enough to help her."

"Then how about going into town with me?" He felt her body tense under his touch. "Halloween night, after the trick-or-treating, Michael and Jes are having a party. It's going to be small, mostly others from the hospital. Ryan will be there, so will the Winterbloom owners Chloe, Jordan, and their daughter."

"I don't know." She bit her lip, nervous.

"It's the perfect chance to test the waters in a protected environment, and there will be other children Abbi can play with. You don't have to make the decision now, just think about it." He gently squeezed her leg. "Instead, how about the three of us take a ride into town today?"

"Why?"

"I have to go to the office to get the medication. You could come with me. You can see how much Clearwater has changed and it will be a good way to entertain Abbi without having her overdo it. I won't be long at the office and you don't even have to get out of the truck. It will be the first step in the right direction."

"Let's see how Abbi feels when she wakes up. She might not be up to it."

He smirked. "That sounds like an excuse."

"Maybe a little," she admitted over the rim of her coffee cup. "I'm not ashamed to say I'm terrified of the idea."

"I'll be there and I promise everything will be okay. Trust me." He rubbed his hand along the top of her leg, not high enough to be questionable but to give her comfort to ease the anxiousness rising within her.

"It might be crazy but I do trust you."

He couldn't stop himself from leaning forward; he wanted to kiss her.

"Mommy," Abbi called from her room.

"I should check on her." She rose and headed for the bedroom.

"While you do that, I'll make breakfast." He stood, taking his coffee with him. He'd finish it and pour himself another while he cooked. Walking around the sofa to the open kitchen he couldn't help but remember how much he despised coffee before medical school. The long hours studying and then his internship had changed his tastes. Coffee had become a lifeline and the only way he could start a day. Without at least a cup, if not more, his brain refused to come out of the fog and focus.

He pulled open the refrigerator door, taking in the contents, before deciding to make French toast. It was an easy dish Jes had taught him when he was still in medical school. At least he knew he couldn't screw up French toast while his thoughts were on other things. Or at least on one woman—Ella.

* * *

"Morning darling." Ella smiled at the sight of her daughter curled up in the middle of the full bed, the blankets pulled around her waist.

"Can I get up?"

"In a bit, Doctor Macis needs to take out your IV first." She same to sit next to her daughter. "You're looking better. How do you feel?"

"Okay, my chest still hurts." As if to emphasize that, Abbi's small body shook with a coughing fit.

"You know Mommy loves you, right?"

"Yeah." Abbi leaned back against the pillows and brought her light brown teddy that had been Ella's when she was a child to sit on her lap. "What's wrong? Are you in trouble with Ryan again?"

"No." She smirked, thinking of the last fight she had with Ryan before Abbi got sick. Like all the others it was about them living out in the woods and what it was doing to her daughter. Ryan's words haunted her: *How will she handle the first day of school if she's never even been into town?* "Do you ever wish you had someone else to play with?"

"Like a little sister? Will you give me one?"

"No, sweetie, we've talked about this." They had been through this a few times over the last few weeks, ever since the bedtime story that had a baby sister in it. Now all Abbi wanted was a sister. That was something Ella couldn't give her without a man, and that was most likely never going to happen. "I was thinking more like a friend."

"I don't know, they might try to take Mr. Bear from me. Or break my toys. Though it might be fun to play hide and seek with someone else."

"It is sweetie, it is." Ella wasn't happy about this sudden revelation her reclusiveness was denying Abbi a lot of what she'd experienced as a child. With a deep breath to calm her rolling stomach, she decided it was time to at least try for her daughter's sake. "Doctor Macis needs to go into town for more medication for you, and he asked us to ride with him. Would you like that?"

Her little head bobbed up and down in excitement. "Can Mr. Bear go with us?"

"I don't see why not. You stay in bed and play with him while I help the doctor with breakfast then we'll take your IV out and get ready." She stood up and took a look around Abbi's room. If it wasn't for the few toys, mostly dolls and stuffed animal scattered around the room, no one would know it was a child's room. The walls were a warm gray, event he full size bed was bland with a quilt that her grandmother made years ago. Nothing like that room Ella had as a child.

She turned on her heels and escaped the room before she cried in front of him. *I'm screwing up raising my baby girl. Damn it, what's wrong with me?*

As she came back into the living room, James turned to look at her, a suspicious glint in his eye. "You okay? You look pale, you're not coming down with something, are you?"

She averted her eyes, then let out the words she could no longer hold in. "For years I've kept on my rose-colored glasses…" She scoffed. "I never truly understood the consequences for my actions." Leaning against the back of the sofa, she watched him, waiting for his response. "Shit, this revelation sucks."

"Sometimes we have to have an eye-opening experience in order to live the life that we were meant to have." He flipped the French toast before continuing. "Take me for example. I lived for my work in Denver, and that's what made me a partner in the practice. The long hours with my own patients, covering for the senior partners when they wanted time off, handling extra hospital shifts or rounds. It all added up and when Jessi moved here I realized if something didn't change, I'd end up like our father."

"So that's why you moved here?"

He nodded. "I was looking into positions when Michael suggested I come on as his partner so he could spend more time with Jessi and the twins. It was perfect. It gave me a less stressful work environment, and enabled me to be close to my nieces."

"I don't think this is going to turn out as well as things did for you." She frowned and dug her fingers into the fabric of the sofa. "I'm a terrible mother."

He piled the last of the French toast onto a plate, then set the tongs aside before going to her. "You're not. You're raising a wonderful little girl. You've worked with her to begin her education, and she's further along than most children her age. That's something to be proud of." He laid his hand over hers.

"Look at her room. Does that look like any little girl's room you've ever seen? She doesn't have any friends. What kind of mother does *this* to her child?"

"You're doing what you think is right by her. That's all any parent can do."

"Maybe you and Ryan are right. Maybe I need to at least travel into town to socialize Abbi. Or maybe I should consider going to Cheyenne like my parents asked. It might be the only way for me to put the past behind me."

"Come here." He placed his hands on her hips, drawing their bodies so close they were almost touching. "Facing the past is the best thing, and once you do that you can begin to make a better life for you and Abbi. I can help you with that…if you'll allow me."

"I admit I miss having a life. Going to Express Ohh's to satisfy my coffee addiction…then I always used to browse the Happy Ever After Bookstore for the newest read. Seeing friends…going to the different activities at the lake, skiing, and snowboarding in Jackson Hole. I want Abbi to experience all the things I did growing up."

"Then let me help you give them to her. Take this ride into town with me, it's the first step in getting your life back. Then maybe we can go to the Halloween festival at the lake, I'm sure Abbi would love it. She can experience the carnival rides, all the delicious food, and you can see no one blames you. All while I'm by your side."

"Why? Why do you want to help us?"

He caressed along the curve of her hips, gently, so as not to scare her off. "Have you ever felt a connection between someone you just met…but you knew they were special?" She froze at his touch, tentative, nervous. "That's how I feel about you and Abbi. Last night, sitting in front of the fire, I got to know you more than anyone else in my life. I told you things Jes or anyone else doesn't even know."

Her heart skipped a beat, and fear tightened her stomach. She had a feeling she knew where this was going, but it excited and terrified her. "What are you saying?"

"That you are special to me and I want to see where this goes. I won't pressure you, but you're not going to be able to push me away like you tried to do yesterday."

"Like yesterday?" Her brows squinted together in confusion.

"When Michael said I was doing this out of charity, you were ready to send me on my way. The only thing that stopped you was that Abbi needed medical attention." He paused as if waiting for her to deny it before he continued. "You're frightened, and I understand, but I'm not going to hurt you."

"Isn't that what they all say? No one scares their prey by telling them what they're going to do to them."

"Is that what you think, that you're my prey?" He leaned down until he could press his forehead against hers.

"No, I just meant…" She kept her hands on the sofa, her body trembling, even though she wanted to wrap her arms around him as he held her.

"I'm not sure how to convince you I'm not like every other man you've known." He moved his hands up her back, pressing her a little closer to him. "You have to trust someone and I'm asking to be that person. Otherwise, we're both going to lose out on something special."

"Not every man, just Josh. He screwed with my head and it's hard to trust anyone after all he put me through. Even after years of having Ryan visit, I'm still cautious of him."

"That couldn't have anything to do with the fact that he nags you to come back to town? Or that he could take your daughter away if he thought she was being neglected or in danger because of your lifestyle choice?"

She swallowed the lump in her throat. "You could do that too."

"No, I don't have that power, but you have to know I wouldn't. Raising a child isn't easy but I think you're doing a good job." He wrapped his arms tighter around her, closing the last distance between them until he had her wrapped in a hug. "I promise you everything is going to be fine. We're going to get through this together. Abbi, you…and me."

She let her head rest against his chest because she wanted to believe him. Trusting him would take everything in her, and if he let her down it would tear her apart. After Josh, she thought she had nothing left to give, but now she wanted to find that part deep within her she had hidden away. She wanted to trust James, to believe in him, to allow everything to fall into place. The question was, could she do it?

Small Town Doctor

Chapter Seven

James strolled from the office with the medication in hand, feeling relaxed and more carefree than he had in months. The ride into town had gone smoothly. Ella was surprised by how little had changed since her last visit, while Abbi was filled with excitement. He took his time, making passes on the side streets so she could see the different businesses. The only place he avoided was On the Rocks, not wanting to make her think about what happened there almost five years ago. Instead, he kept it pleasant, even taking a drive past Clearwater Lake to see the first rides being erected for the festival.

He glanced around the empty parking lot, wondering if it would be too much if he suggested they sat in the gazebo for a while, letting Abbi play in the grass. When he saw a few hospital employees at a nearby table he decided to save the idea for another day. He waved to another doctor who was getting out of his car across the parking lot before he opened the truck door and hopped in.

"Did you get what you needed?" Ella asked, her gaze scanning the parking lot. She still had a smile on her face, and that was what mattered most to him.

"Sure did." He tossed the small paper bag of medication into the armrest compartment. "What do you girls say, want to drive around town some more? I can take you past Michael and Jessi's, and my rental house is just down the road from them."

"Can we, Mommy?"

"Why not." She grinned back at her daughter. "As long as James doesn't mind."

"Please, Doctor Macis." Ella begged, leaning forward from where she was nestled on the back seat.

"Little one, your wish is my command." He smirked. Everything was perfect. He shoved the truck into drive and started to pull out of the parking lot, when his cell phone rang. In the pit of his stomach he knew he shouldn't answer it; whoever was on the other end was about to spoil this perfect moment, but as a doctor he couldn't ignore it.

He pulled to the side of the exit and tugged his cell phone off his belt. "I've got to take this." Ella nodded as he brought it to his ear. "Doctor Macis."

"James, this is Jordan Shepherd, I need your help." The Winterbloom Bed and Breakfast owner's voice came through the speaker with a touch urgency.

"Is it Bianca?"

"No, Bianca and Chloe are fine. I have a friend and a former Marine, Sergeant Gioven Sparks, staying here at Winterbloom. I need your help with him."

"I'm a pediatrician, I don't know what I can do to help. What's wrong with him?"

"His last deployment was hairy and he's turned to the bottle to help him cope. I need to get him out of On the Rocks, and Ryan's on police business. I don't want Chloe there, but if I can't find anyone else, that's what I'm going to have to do…unless you can help."

"No, if he's a drunk former Marine you're going to need more than just Chloe. Leave her home with Bianca and I'll meet you there. I'm at the hospital, give me five minutes."

"See you there, I'm already in the parking lot." Jordan ended the call.

James locked his phone screen and clipped it back onto his belt. "I've got to help Jordan, I can leave you in my office if you'd prefer."

"Where at?"

"On the Rocks." He saw the fear shine in her eyes. "You don't have to go in, you can wait in the car or wait here, but I need an answer."

"We'll go. There's no reason for you to come back here for us…but we'll wait in the car."

He shoved the truck back in drive. "I'll try to make it quick." Knowing the sacrifice she was making, he reached across the seat to lay his hand on her leg.

"I know you will." She placed her hand over his and gave it a gentle squeeze. "Are you sure two of you can handle a drunk Marine? Maybe you should call for additional help."

"We'll be fine. Once we get him under control, the bar owner, Daniel Bridge, will help if we need him to. He's probably tired of hearing Gioven's problems as he downs a bottle of whiskey. Daniel is a bartending therapist…at least according to most of the town's drinkers." He took the alley from the hospital over to Queen Street, where On the Rocks was just about on the outskirts of town.

"What's whiskey?" Abbi questioned as she rocked Mr. Bear in her lap.

"It's a drink for people Mommy's age."

"Nasty stuff." He glanced in the review mirror back at her, wrinkling his nose in distaste. Turning his attention back to the road he made the turn into the parking lot and immediately spotted Jordan leaning against his truck.

The truck took to the gravel parking lot with ease and he pulled up next to Jordan before putting it in park. "I'll be right back." He squeezed her hand before grabbing the door handle. He hated to leave her in the one spot he knew brought back bad memories, but he couldn't let Jordan handle this on his own.

"Sorry, man. I hoped to get Ryan to help, since Cameron and J.C. are teaching a class at Clearwater Combat and Guns," Jordan called to him as he came around the front of the truck.

"No problem. Let's see if we can get him out without causing a scene and disrupting Daniel's lunch crowd."

"Who's the woman?" Jordan nodded to the truck where Ella was staring at the bar, her eyes wide.

"Ella Carmichael and her daughter Abbi."

"The Carmichaels from the mountain?" Jordan raised an eyebrow at him, shock evident in his gaze. "Ryan's been trying to get them into town for years. How'd you do it?"

He had a number of smart-ass comments in mind but he wanted this over so he could get back to Ella before she could talk herself into blocking him out again. "I thought we had someone we needed to rescue from the bar."

"Yes, right, Gioven." Jordan turned toward the bar while James glanced back at the truck.

He wanted to slip back into the truck and wrap his arms around Ella, to ease the discomfort she was feeling. If bringing her to On the Rocks destroyed what he accomplished already, he'd have a battle that was twice as hard. She'd close in on herself until he had to chisel away at the outer edge, begging her to open up again. There was no chance it would be as easy as the first time.

Damn it, I'm risking her to help someone else. She's supposed to be my top priority.

* * *

The two story brick building that housed On the Rocks stared back at Ella almost in a taunting manner, reminding her of the last time she'd visited the bar and the horrors of that night. Her thoughts took her back, changing the beautiful day into the dark wintery night. Everything crumbled away until it looked like it did then.

She remembered staggering out of the car, her head splitting, blood spilling down her face. The first thing she remembered seeing as she came out of the bar was the little red truck they'd come in parked across from the exit, but Josh's friends were nowhere in sight. A moment of relief filled her with the knowledge she hadn't been left behind. That was until she scanned the parking lot and found Josh hunched over the man he had been fighting with in the bar. She'd tried to stop him from following the man to the parking lot, but what she received for her efforts was a punch to the jaw that sent her staggering backward until she fell into the corner of the bar and hit her head. That was when everything went black. While she lay unconscious on the barroom floor, Josh was out in the parking lot fighting. That showed the concern he had for her.

"Josh!" She pushed her way through the crowd when someone grabbed her arm to stop her. She wasn't sure who had been there that night; the only one she could recall to this day had been the bartender, Daniel. Everyone else was just a blur.

She was trying to fight her way from the guy's grasp when Josh looked over at her. His face and shirt were covered in blood as he continued to beat the man's head into the ground. What she saw in his eyes, the pure hatred, rage, and the excitement of what he was doing, scared her enough to recoil, to stop fighting the hold the stranger had on her arm.

Torn between trying to stop Josh and terrified his rage would turn on her, she was frozen in place. Over and over, Josh slammed the man against the pavement. People shrieked for him to stop, but no one dared touch him. She couldn't figure out why until she saw two others on the ground. One with a bullet hole in his chest and the other with a bleeding skull. What had happened while she was unconscious?

"Mommy?" Abbi shook Ella's shoulder with her small hand, pulling her back from her thoughts. "Mommy, are you okay?"

"I…" She fought to push the memories away and find her voice. "I'm fine."

"You're shivering. Do you want my blanket, Mommy?"

She looked down at her hands and sure enough she was shaking, though it wasn't from the cold like her daughter thought. It was from the memories, a chill that couldn't be chased away by turning on the heater or adding an extra layer. "Thanks, sweetie, but I'm okay."

"Look, he's coming back." Abbi pointed to the bar's main entrance where James and Jordan were struggling to get Gioven out of the bar. He fought them with every step as they practically carried him out.

"Abbi, I want you to stay in this truck. Don't you dare get out! Do you understand? I'm going to help." She didn't wait for Abbi's answer; she'd always been a well-behaved child who listened when Ella told her something. Before she could talk herself out of it, she slipped from the truck, shut the door behind her, and crossed the parking lot.

"Ella, get back in the truck," James hollered over Gioven moans.

"Let me help." She closed the distance between them.

"H-hey, hey, beautiful, care to have a drink with me?" Gioven leaned toward her. "Mmm, you s-smell delicious."

"Gioven." James growled, making it clear he was pushing the limits.

She laid her hand on Gioven's chest to help steady him. "I think you've had enough."

"I'm s-still awake…so I haven't had enough." His voice was thick and his words slurred.

They leaned Gioven against the truck as Jordan opened the passenger door. "Oh-oh, b-beautiful, you deserve someone better than me. I'm broken, a...a useless shell of a man."

"Hey, now." She cupped the side of his cheek, tipping his head back to look at her. "There's none of that. You're an attractive man and any woman would be honored to have your affections."

"Just not you." His head fell back against the truck with a thump. "Because I'm broken."

"No, because there's someone else. At least I think...it's all happened so quickly." She glanced at James before forcing her attention back to Gioven. "Can I give you some good advice?"

"Sure, beautiful, but I can't promise I'll take it."

"You can't run from your problems." When he started to interrupt her, she placed her finger over his lips. "I tried for years, hiding up in the mountains. Do you know today is the first time I've been in town after nearly five years of living in a cabin in the woods? Alcohol or being a recluse, neither of those take the problems away. I don't know how much help I'd be, but if you'd ever want to talk..."

"There's no chance I can make you change your mind and come home with me instead of him?"

"No. I think what's best is you go back and get some sleep." Her heart broke for the sadness she saw in his eyes. It wasn't sorrow because she was rejecting him, but because of what he saw during his time as a Marine. He was suffering with post-traumatic stress disorder and needed help. "I'd like to come talk to you once you're sober, if you'd be willing call James's cell, Jordan has the number, and he'll get the message to me."

"Come on, Gioven, let's get you into the truck." Jordan nodded to the open door. "Get in and I'll drive you back to Winterbloom so you can sleep."

"What about my truck?" Gioven nodded toward the black pick-up across the parking lot.

"Give me the keys." James held out his hand. "I'll drive it back."

"What about *your* truck?" Jordan asked as Gioven handed the keys over.

"If you're okay with it, I could drive and follow you." When everyone turned to her, looking surprised. "Don't look so shocked, I still have my license."

"Okay. We'll follow behind you and leave your truck at Winterbloom, as long as you don't drive drunk."

Gioven agreed as he climbed into the passenger seat and rested his head against the back of the seat. "Thank you, though I think the beautiful woman should be driving me home instead."

"I've got my daughter in James's truck. Now don't give Jordan any problems." She shut the door and stepped back only to find the other two men watching her. "What?"

"He was a belligerent drunk and then you showed up."

"Jordan's right, we couldn't have done this without you." James wrapped his arm around her waist, pulling her closer to him. "Thank you."

She leaned her head against his shoulder when her gaze caught a woman exiting the bar. Daniel was trying to stop her but was having no luck. They were headed right for her and the men, making the hairs on the back of her neck stand on end. Something was wrong, she could just feel it.

"How dare you come back here!"

"Doris." Daniel tried to take hold of the woman's arm and stop her, but she managed to slip out of his reach.

James slipped his arm from Ella's waist and stepped in front of her. Not completely blocking her from view, but making it clear he'd protect her if things got out of hand. Jordan mimicked him, while Ella stood there wondering who the woman was.

"How dare you, the two of you? Especially you, Jordan, I expected more from you. She helped *kill* my brother. He was ex-military just like you, and now you're going to protect *her*."

Just like that, the pieces fell into place, and her stomach twisted until it was one big ball of knots. Doris Bagwell, the sister of the man Josh murdered.

"Now, Doris, I was there that night and we both know that's not what happened." Daniel's voice, brimming with a heavy country twang, cut in. "She was as much of a victim as your brother."

"*Victim?*" Doris swung her body around to face the bartender, her fists balled as if she was ready to fight anyone who disagreed with her. "She *brought* him here."

She had to give Daniel credit that he didn't back down to the woman's rage.

"That might be the case, but that doesn't mean she's responsible any more than you're responsible for your brother's actions. Those two men had a disagreement they decided to settle with their fists. The few who were here that night tried to break it up and two of them nearly died."

Ella took a deep breath. "Doris..." When the woman turned to her, hatred in her eyes, she paused, trying to find the courage to continue. "You're right...I brought him to Clearwater. But I didn't know he'd do anything like that. I'd have never brought him here if I thought he was capable of murder."

Daniel gestured to Ella. "She was unconscious on the bar floor when the fight started," he reasoned. "You remember that, don't you? Damn it, Doris, you were the one who applied ice to her head."

"The man who attacked your brother was not the man I thought I knew," Ella said, her voice soft. "I'm sorry for what happened and—"

"Don't you think she feels guilty enough?" Jordan said boldly. "She's been in hiding since that happened, letting the guilt eat at her. The first time she comes back into town, you rush at her like you've got something to settle with her."

"What do you know about it, Jordan? You were still off servicing your country when this happened. You weren't here, either, Doctor...and you seem very willing to protect her. Do you have something to gain from it?" Doris countered.

"You're right," Jordan began, "I wasn't here, but I've heard enough about what happened—"

James cut him off. "I've gotten to know her, and like Jordan I know what happened. I'm not willing to let you make a stupid mistake because you've had a few drinks. I suggest you go back inside." He nodded toward the bar.

"He's right, Doris, come on." Daniel laid his hand on her arm.

"Doris, I met your brother a few times when I was in town, he was a good man," Ella said. "I'm very sorry for your loss. It's a tragedy what happened that night, one I'll never forget." She didn't say what she was thinking, that it was a tragedy she'd finally come to realize wasn't her fault. She couldn't have controlled Josh's actions any more than she could control the weather.

She might never be able to forget what happened, but she'd begun to put it behind her. It was time to move on with her life, and maybe love again. James had shown her there was so much she was missing. For her and her daughter's sakes, she was reclaiming her life with both hands—and this time, she wouldn't back down.

Chapter Eight

James wasn't sure when he had made the decision, but somehow after dropping off Gioven's truck at Winterbloom, he'd decided to swing past his house before going back to Ella's cabin. They needed to give Abbi dinner so she could have her pill, and he didn't want their time together to end. While Abbi dozed on his sofa, he had Ella to himself.

He came up behind her as she stood by the window and wrapped his arms around her waist. "I'm proud of how you handled things with Gioven and then Doris."

"She lost her brother because of a decision I made."

"No." He kept his arm around her but turned her slightly so she was in front of him. "Her brother is dead because of a decision he and Josh made. They chose to take the fight outside and then Josh, *not* you, chose to commit murder instead of stepping away from the fight when it was clear he had won. None of that is your fault."

"Somewhere in my thoughts I know you're right, but there's that nagging guilt reminding me I brought him to Clearwater. Otherwise, he wouldn't have been here and this would have never happened, but then again...*she'd* have never happened. She's the light of my life." She looked past him to Abbi.

"She's worth it all, isn't she?" He smirked. "You've got an amazing little girl, and as I told you before you have nothing to worry about. She's got to be the calmest child I've met, no temper hiding under the surface."

"Are you sure?"

He nodded. "We spoke while you were getting ready, and I can see it in how she acts. You have nothing to worry about."

"What a relief." She let out a sigh. "I guess that means I don't have an excuse for hiding in the mountains any longer."

"I never said you had to leave your home, just come into town sometimes. Let Abbi play with the other children." He ran his hand up her back. "Though it would seem as if you already agreed to come back to town since you offered to visit Gioven while he's staying in Clearwater."

"He's running from what he saw while he was deployed. I can't help him with that, but maybe I can use my experiences to help him get away from the booze. I thought about turning to the bottle myself to help ease the nightmares of what happened. What saved me was I found out I was pregnant. I couldn't drown my sorrows in booze and hurt an innocent child. He doesn't have that but he needs help, more help than I can give him."

"Jordan mentioned he's been trying to get him to see a therapist to help him through the PTSD, but Gioven refuses. He seems to like you, maybe you can convince him."

"I'll try. He seems like a nice guy who just lost his way."

"Unfortunately, many of our military men and woman who come back from deployments suffer with some degree of PTSD. Many of them go untreated, either because of shame, embarrassment, or they just don't understand the options available for them."

"I'll see what I can do for him."

He decided this was as good as time as any to broach the subject that had been on his mind since the parking lot excitement. "Earlier you deflected his advances by telling him there was someone else. Were you being truthful, or using it as a way to sidestep his advances without hurting him?"

"I just met you…but I feel this connection to you. Maybe it's because I've been alone for so long, or maybe it's because last night I got to know you better than I've know anyone my whole life. Either way I'm willing to explore it. I just ask that you have patience with me."

"I will as long as you don't shut me out." He kissed the top of her forehead. "Since I think we'll be seeing quite a bit of each other, you should explain to Abbi she can call me James. I don't want to hear Doctor Macis all the time while I'm off duty."

He couldn't believe how the last two days had turned out. He'd gone from a medical call he wasn't sure about, to finding a woman he was beginning to fall for—not to mention a little girl he was very fond of. It wouldn't be long before Abbi had him wrapped around her little finger; the adorable little blonde was hard to say no to.

I'm a goner for sure.

* * *

Night had settled over the sleepy town as they made the final climb toward the mountain home. Ella sat there feeling quite happy with herself. She had made it through a full day in town, faced her fears of On the Rocks, helped a man, confronted Doris, and made progress with James. It had been a day of challenges, but in the end everything worked out better than she could have hoped. She could pat herself on the back for how many challenges she had overcome in such a short time. Now she didn't want it to end. She didn't want to see him drive away from them. Would he come back? Or had their brief encounter been a fluke?

"Ella, there's a silver SUV in the driveway. Do you know them or do you want me to turn around?"

"Shit." She leaned forward in the seat to get a better look at the SUV, and her fears came true. So much for the perfect day, now she had to face two of her biggest opponents. *Her parents.* During the past few years, every time she spoke to her parents it turned into a fight. One she didn't want to have in front of James or with Abbi in hearing range.

"I can turn around."

"It's no use, they'll only follow. You're about to meet Mr. and Mrs. Carmichael. My parents." She let out a low growl. "If I find out who called them I'm going to have their head on my wall."

"What?"

"Last time they made an impromptu visit it was because town gossip started swirling again and someone from Clearwater called my parents. They showed up at my door at two in the morning." She turned to look back at Abbi. "I damn near shot them that night."

"What?" He asked again as they neared her parents' waiting SUV.

"You're beginning to sound like a stuck CD," she joked. "Come on, do you think I would really be out here all alone with my daughter if I didn't have protection? There are animals in these woods, not to mention anyone could show up and there's no way to get help. I don't have a phone and the cell I have for emergencies only works about a mile up the mountain."

He stopped the truck behind the SUV just as two people started to climb out. "No, I figured you had a gun, I guess I'm just shocked you almost shot your parents. I'll have to give you some kind of warning when I come to visit."

With the truck in park, she tipped her head back to her daughter. "Could you take Abbi into the house and put her to bed? Whatever brought my parents here isn't something she needs to overhear."

"Sure." He palmed the keys before placing his other hand over the door handle. "By the way, no one listens to CDs any longer, it's all digital music now. You're going to have to update you smartass comments if you're going to face the real world."

With that he managed to lighten the mood and ease the building tension. "James..." She paused for a moment, waiting for him to turn back to her. "I know we discussed you staying to keep an eye on Abbi again, but I understand if you'd like to leave. My parents are a handful, and she's doing okay."

"Does that mean you'd like me to leave?"

She glanced toward her parents where they stood waiting by the rear of the SUV. "No, I'd rather you stay but—"

"Then consider me your bodyguard." He reached over and laid his hand on hers. "It's going to be okay."

"You don't know my parents. Whatever brought them here means only one thing, they came willing to fight for what they think is right." She laced her fingers between his and soaked up the comfort of having someone at her side. "Delay will only make Mom angry, so let's do this."

"Once I get Abbi into bed I'll come back out." He opened the door, stepped out, and made his way around the truck while she took one last moment for herself. She needed to prepare to deal with her parents.

She wasn't sure, but it seemed as if they had become more difficult to deal with now that she lived life on her own terms. They wanted to control her, force her to live the life they thought she should have. Up until that night with Josh, she had been willing to please them, but after she witnessed the murder everything changed, and her parents didn't like it one bit.

"This is my life and I have the right to live it however I want." With a dose of encouragement, she grabbed hold of the door handle. "I can do this."

"After facing your fears today, I know you can handle this, and I'll be right there with you once I get the little one to bed," he whispered as he lifted Abbi into his arms.

The minute she stepped out of the truck, her mother was on her. "Ella Louise Carmichael, where the hell have you been? You've had your father and I sitting out here for the last two hours."

"Mom, if I had known you were coming I'd have made sure I was here." She stepped toward her parents, taking their full attention so James could get Abbi inside before she awoke. They'd question who he was, and there was no way she could skip that part, but Abbi didn't need to need to be awake for this.

"How was I supposed to let you know we were coming when you live like this? Damn it, Ella, you need to get over this crazy of idea of living like your father's parents and come home with us. This is no way to raise a child."

"Mom, we've had this discussion before. I'm staying. As for raising a child, Dad was raised like this and he turned out fine." She was tired of going over the same thing every time they saw each other.

"He's a man, hard work is one thing for them," she countered, "but it's different for Abbi. Times have changed."

Her father, Dale, came to stand beside her mother and laid a hand on her shoulder, but she shook it off.

"Dad also has a sister—"

Her mother cut her off. "You don't have to remind me of his family. Unlike you, I see his sister and the rest of our family regularly. You're the only one who chooses to live like a scared cat."

"Mom, please." She let out a deep breath and tried to hold onto the calm that was quickly slipping away. "It's been a long day and I don't want to fight. What are you doing here?"

"We received a call that Abbi was sick and the Sheriff had to make a special call out here because of it. I won't have my grandchild hauled off to some state home for children because you can't care for her, so your father and I decided to give you a choice."

Ella let out a soft growl, anger heating her blood. "How about I give *you* a choice? Either you let me live my life as I want or leave me alone."

"That's exactly what we're going to do." Her mother looked back at her husband, who shook his head in obvious discomfort before she pushed forward. "We've come here asking for you to sign custody of Abbi over to us."

"You what?" Ella couldn't believe what she heard.

"If you don't sign the paperwork we'll be forced to take you to court to get it. I won't see my granddaughter raised like this any longer. She's sick and you won't take her to the doctor. That's the final straw."

"You'll do no such thing." She'd fight with everything in her to keep her daughter.

James came to stand behind her, his hand on the small of her back. "It would seem you've been brought here by someone who doesn't have all the information."

"Who would you be?" Bea raised an eyebrow at him in question.

"Doctor James Macis, I'm a pediatrician here in Clearwater and I've been treating Abbi." James rubbed his thumb under her shirt until he was touching skin.

"Seems like there's more going on than just doctor-patient relationships."

"That's our business," she snapped before giving her reply proper thought. "James, these are my parents, Bea and Dale."

"We've given Ella numerous chances to return to Cheyenne with us but she's determined to stay in this run-down cabin." Bea raised her voice. "No longer will I let Abbi be victim to it. I've come to take her to a proper home." She stepped toward the cabin but James cut her off.

"I can't allow that."

"You what?" Bea spun to face him. Her wide eyes made it clear she couldn't believe he was trying to stop her.

"As her doctor I can't advise that kind of travel. It's nearly seven hours and she needs her rest."

"That's not the point." Everyone looked at Ella, except James who pressed himself closer to her as if trying to give her comfort through his touch.

"Then what is?" Bea questioned.

"She's my daughter and she's not going anywhere." She glanced toward her father who had remained silent through all of this. "Dad, what do you think of this? You were raised here. Do you think I'm neglecting Abbi? Do you really want to take her away from me and raise her yourself?"

Dale shuffled his weight back and forth from one leg to the other, unable to meet Ella's gaze. He had always been too easy-going, letting Bea control everything. Whatever she said or wanted he went along with, even if it wasn't what he wanted. He was a good husband and a great father but she had always wished he had more of a backbone when it came to her mother. Now she was putting him on the spot, hoping he'd help her when she needed it the most.

"Dad…"

"I heard you, Ella." He shoved his hands into the pocket of his slacks and finally looked in her direction, still avoiding direct eye contact with her. "No. Abbi deserves to be with you and I think you're doing a fine job. Yes, you could socialize her more, but as you said I was raised here. My sister was my only playmate for many years and we were homeschooled." He looked to his wife. "I don't want to take Abbi back to Cheyenne. We've done our job as parents, now it's Ella's turn. We make the trips here to see them, Abbi is a happy and healthy little girl."

"She's not healthy now, and what's being done about it? The girl couldn't even walk under her own steam into the house," Bea raged.

"I'd say she's taking care of that. Doctor…what did you say your name was?"

"Please call me James." He reached forward and shook hands with Dale, which seemed to annoy Bea even more. "Abbi is being taken care of. She has pneumonia but I've given her medication through an IV last night to get things started, and she's on an antibiotic. I carried her inside because she's had a full day and she's tired." James laced his fingers between Ella's. "We've been in town."

"Town?" Bea questioned.

"Yes, Mother, town." Ella couldn't help but raise her voice with the rage she was feeling. Leave it to her mother to question Ella's ability to be a parent, only to be concerned with a minor detail. "Though I'm not sure you're asking the right question. What about your granddaughter's health? Or do you not care that she has pneumonia?"

"I care or I wouldn't have traveled here, now would I?" Bea snapped.

James ran his hand up Ella's arm. "Abbi stirred a little while I was putting her to bed, why don't you go and tuck her in?"

"If you're staying, you can come inside, but if you don't keep your voice down so Abbi can rest I'll ask you to leave." She slipped her hand into his, until she found the comfort she sought.

She was thankful for the out he gave her; it would allow her to get herself in the right frame of mind to battle whatever her mother threw at her. Willing to do most anything to keep him there, if only for one more night, she leaned into him. "Come with me."

Small Town Doctor

Chapter Nine

James shut Abbi's bedroom door behind them, to give them a moment before they had to face her parents again. The thin door between them was enough to ease some of the tension he'd witnessed in Ella since they arrived. He wanted to go to her and wrap his arm around her again, to feel her warm skin under his touch, but he wasn't sure where they stood. He'd done it in front of her parents because he felt she needed it, and because he thought it would cause them to back off. He wasn't sure he succeeded, but he was willing to work on it harder if it forced them to ease off of Ella.

Ella stood facing the bed where Abbi was sleeping, her back to him. "She's asleep."

"I know." He stepped closer to make sure she heard him as he whispered. "She never woke but I thought you needed a moment."

"Thank you." She let out a sign and rotated her shoulders. "For everything. You didn't have to go up against my parents like you did. You could have dropped us off here to deal with them and gone back to town. When I was growing up, anytime my mother started about anything everyone always took off. She's like a dog with a bone she won't give up until she has what she wants."

"Hey now." He laid his hand on her shoulder. "I'm not leaving, unless you want me to. Which brings us to a very important question."

"Which is?"

"How do you want things to go with your parents? I'll admit seeing your mother threatening to take your daughter away worked my nerves, so I stepped in. Maybe I shouldn't have, and with most I wouldn't have, but you're not most." He used his hand on her shoulder to turn her around to face him. "Your mother believes there's something going on between us."

"Isn't there?" Her voice was soft as her hand fell against his chest.

"I hope so, but let's say more than what has happened so far. You had to have noticed how she watched the touches we shared."

"Oh, I saw." She smirked up at him.

"I need to know how you want to handle the rest of the time your parents are here. Do you want me to leave?"

"Do you want to leave? What about Abbi?"

Unable to hold back his desires any longer he leaned down, closing the distance between them to claim her lips. The sweet honey from the tea she drank earlier still lingered there. He kept the kiss sweet, gently pulling her bottom lip between his teeth, just enough to show the desire he had for her but not enough to scare her—at least he hoped. When he pulled back her eyes were still closed as if she was trying to savor the moment. "Does that tell you what I want?"

"Umm." She finally opened her eyes.

"I want to stay, but if you want me to leave so you can deal with your parents I'll come back in the morning to check on Abbi."

"No, stay." She ran her hand up his chest. "I guess I can't hide out in here all night so let's see about getting rid of them."

"I don't think it's going to be that easy. Bea seems determined, even if Dale isn't. She's really against you living here, isn't she?"

"She always has been. At first she thought I needed some time so she didn't fight as much, but about a month before Abbi was born she started and hasn't stopped." She glanced back at her daughter's sleeping form. "I might not have been the perfect parent so far but I've done what I thought was right."

"That's what matters. After all, children don't come with a manual, you have to rely on your gut instincts and go with that. Abbi is a great little girl. Once she's feeling better, we'll take her into town and let her play with kids her own age. We'll face that together just like we're going to face your parents." He slipped his hand into hers. "Ready?"

"Never." She tried to laugh it off but couldn't quite manage it. "Let's do this before I crawl into bed with Abbi and try to forget they're here."

"Oh no, you're not leaving me alone to deal with them." He shook his head. "Let's convince them we have things under control and I'll reward you once they're gone." He let his thoughts wander for a moment as he pulled open the door. Ideas of getting her naked were short lived as Bea shot up from the sofa and picked up right where they'd left off.

"I demand some answers. What the hell is going on between the two of you?"

"Mom…"

He squeezed her hand. "It okay. Bea, things are still new between us but I care for her. We're taking things slow while she finds her own footing in this."

"You care for her?" Bea's eyes widened. "If that's true then how can you stand there while she lives like this? While Abbi suffers?" She waved her arms around the small cabin as if that explained everything.

"You might have different views on how Ella raises Abbi but it's her decision. She's a grown woman and she's not placing Abbi in any danger, otherwise other measures would have already been taken."

"Mom, I've told you before this is my life and you need to let me live it how I want. Abbi's growing up learning skills that will carry her through the rest of her life."

"What about learning how to make friends? To play like a child her age should?"

"I grew up on more of a farm than this and we still had time to play," Dale cut in, coming to the rescue. "Chores were a part of the daily schedule, but you've seen Abbi does more than that. Ella has already begun teaching Abbi how to read, her numbers and alphabet. Those are skills others her age haven't even begun yet. Ella is doing a fine job with Abbi. You're only upset because she's not living in Cheyenne with us so you can watch over her like a hawk. Bea, it's time you stop being a mother hen and let Ella and Abbi have their life. We visit almost every month, what more do you want?"

"I want her to move out of your parents' shack. I want her in Cheyenne or at the very least back in Jackson Hole." Bea stated, frowning.

"But that's the life you want for her, not the one she wants." Dale watched his wife for a moment before he looked back to Ella. "It seems things have changed since our last visit. Not only with this *relationship* but also the trip into town." He hesitated on relationship as if he wasn't sure what to call this new development between her and James.

"I guess they have, at least to a point, but that doesn't mean I'm leaving here. This is my home now. I'm not moving back to Jackson Hole, nor am I moving in with you in Cheyenne. Every time you visit I make this clear. Coming here demanding I sign custody of my daughter over was the last straw." She took a deep breath and James squeezed her hand again. She wasn't sure if he was trying to tell her to tread carefully or that he had her back, but either way she pushed forward. "You're my parents and I love you. Abbi needs her grandparents in her life."

"What are you getting at?" Bea asked.

"I can't have this same fight every time, it's not healthy and I won't have Abbi witness it each visit. If you're going to continue visiting, then you need to respect my choices, otherwise I think it might be best to limit your visits."

"You'll what?" Bea shot up from the sofa. "See why I want to take Abbi away from this?" She looked down at Dale. "She's trying to keep us away from our granddaughter."

"No, Bea." Dale rose to stand in front of his wife. "She's trying to keep Abbi away from the *tension* you bring every time you come up here demanding Ella leaves the cabin, and now this latest plot to take Abbi back to Cheyenne. I should have never let you talk me into this. That's it. We're going into town, to our room at Winterbloom, and tomorrow with Ella's permission we'll come back to see them, but then we'll return to Cheyenne alone. We're not taking Abbi, and Ella needs time to see where things go with this relationship. In a few weeks we'll come back for our regular visit."

Ella shuffled her weight between her feet. "You just made the journey here, if you're going to stop bitching about my lifestyle, you can stay."

"I agree with Ella, you don't have to rush off." James nodded toward Abbi's bedroom and added, "If you'll let Abbi rest, it could be good for her to have you visiting. I'm sure she'd love to see her grandparents, have you read to her or something while she's confined to bed."

"You don't want us to leave?" Bea wasn't able to keep the surprise out of her voice.

"No, Mom, I don't want you to leave."

"Then how about we come back in the morning. It's been a long drive, Bea, and I'm tired. I'm sure Ella needs her rest as well, caring for a sick child is tiring." Dale nodded toward the door. "Let's go."

"One last thing." Bea looked at James with full seriousness. "I don't know what's between you and Ella, but I won't stand for you taking advantage of her or this situation."

"Mom," Ella snapped.

"No, Ella, it's okay." He wrapped his arm around her waist. "I have come to care about both Ella and Abbi, so you don't have to worry about me hurting her. Your daughter has a good head on her shoulders, she's not going to let anyone take advantage of her."

Ella turned slightly in his embrace to look at him, as if wondering if he meant what he said. He didn't know what she saw, but whatever she saw on his face made her smile. "James is unlike anyone I've ever met. He's great with Abbi, and has a heart of gold. I can't tell you where things are going between us, but don't get your hopes up because I'm sure it will be slower than your liking."

He snuggled her body against his. "Whatever speed you want things is how we'll take it."

"Let's go, Bea, these two are getting like those romantic movies you makes me watch." Dale grabbed his jacket from the back of the sofa.

"There's one last thing I think you should know." James ran his hand down Ella's arm. "Ella came to the rescue of a soldier today. He's suffering from post-traumatic stress disorder and instead of getting the help he needs he's choosing to fight the pain with alcohol. While another guy and I were struggling to get him into the truck, Ella came over and calmed him. Whatever she said to him got his attention."

"You did this?" Bea took the coat her husband handed her but didn't put it on.

"I didn't think about it when I hopped out of James's truck. I just knew they needed help and I was the only one around. Actually, I told him I'd stop by to see him, so maybe while you're here you can watch Abbi so James can take me into town to see him. I don't know if I can be of any help to him, but maybe I can convince him to see someone who can." She tipped her head to look at him. "That is, if you don't mind."

"Not at all. How about tomorrow after lunch? Unless you're planning to leave—"

Bea looked back at Dale to see if he'd agree to stay, and he nodded. "If Winterbloom has rooms, we'll stay. I just have to be back in Cheyenne on Wednesday because my sister returns from Florida, and I'm supposed to pick her up at the airport."

Bea slipped into her coat. "We'll see you tomorrow and thank you for asking us to watch Abbi while you go into town. It's the first time, and that alone gives me hope."

Ella stepped out of James's embrace and went to her mother. "You have to know that I'm not living here to go against what you want. I just want a life with solitude."

Bea hugged her but didn't say anything. It was Dale who came up to her and wrapped his arm around her. "There's solitude and there's reclusiveness. We just want you to live a happy life, to have friends, and eventually a relationship that will give you someone who's by your side always." He glanced at James before leaning in. "Maybe him?"

"Dad…"

He stopped her by kissing her forehead. "We'll see you in the morning."

James hung back as Ella said goodbye to her parents and wondered what he should do. Abbi didn't need him to stay, she was stable enough that he could go back to his house, but all he wanted to do was to cuddle up with Ella in front of the fire.

With the door shut, Ella turned to face him. "You've met my parents. Does it make you want to run in the opposite direction screaming, like it does me?"

"No, they care about you." He stalked toward her. "Plus I think you're worth having to deal with, even with the worst in any family."

"Is that so?"

"Yes, you are." Now that he stood in front of her, he was able to reach out and place his hands on her hips. "I'm going to kiss you, stop me if you don't want me to."

He leaned closer, pausing just before his lips met hers and looked into her eyes. When she did nothing to stop him, he made good on his promise. He slowly slid his tongue between her lips, exploring her mouth. He finally broke the kiss, leaving them breathless for a moment.

"Stay with me tonight." Her voice was low as she continued to gaze into his eyes.

"I was hoping you'd ask." He tugged her toward the sofa.

"No." She bit her lip as if suddenly nervous. "Come to my bed. I want to feel your arms around me as we cuddle."

"Are you sure?" Even with every ounce of his body wanting to do just what she asked, he didn't want to rush her. She had to be sure this was what she wanted, what she needed.

"I've never been so sure of anything in my life." She led him toward her bedroom. "For the first time in years I feel like I'm living. I don't want that to end. Come to bed and hold me in your arms…just make me feel alive."

Chapter Ten

The chirping of birds in the tree next to Ella's window forced her to stir. She started to roll over to face the window when she collided with someone. Thinking it was Abbi, she forced her eyes open to check on her. Only to find James still peacefully asleep next to her. The night came flooding back. They had cuddled in her bed, talking, until sleep pressed against them, scattering their thoughts and making their eyes flutter shut.

It was the first time she was happy to wake up next to someone else. She could get used to having James beside her, the first thing she saw when she opened her eyes.

Easy girl. She tried to remind herself they just met, but even that wasn't enough to stop the thoughts of having him in her bed every night from spreading. They might have just met but she had come to know him better than anyone else in her life, even her former female friends.

"Morning beautiful." His rough voice, laced with sleep, pulled her from her thoughts. "How long have you been awake?"

"Only a few minutes. I was tempted to curl against your body and fall asleep again."

"Why don't we?" He used the arm that was wrapped around her to pull her back down until her head was resting in the crook of his shoulder, and he kissed her forehead.

"Because my parents will be arriving soon." She reminded him, her hand sliding along his naked chest. "Though a day in bed next to you sounds heavenly."

"I can't promise a whole day in bed once Abbi is back to her normal self, but I think we could arrive at a leisurely lie-in."

She propped herself up on her elbow. "Thank you for staying."

"I'll stay every night if you'll have me." He ran his hand down her back. "Actually I was wondering if you and Abbi would stay with me tonight?"

"What?" She tipped her head. Wasn't the occasional trip to town enough for now?

"Don't look at me with those wide eyes full of fear. I suggested this because Michael and I rotate hospital duty, and this week is mine. I need to be in town in case there's an emergency but I'd like you with me. That way I can keep an eye on Abbi."

"I have a feeling it's less about Abbi and more about getting me out of this cabin." If she was right about that, she didn't like it one bit. To have him use his work as an excuse to manipulate her.

"Okay, it's not about Abbi, but it has nothing to do with this cabin either. It's about having you with me. I realize this is all happening fast, but I'd like to have you stay with me. I want to get to know you better, to feel your warm body next to mine." He leaned up and nuzzled his head into the crook of her shoulder, kissing along her shoulder until he reached the base of her neck.

"I don't want my parents to know." She shook her head, bumping slightly into his. "I sound like a high school girl sneaking out at night, instead of a grown woman with a daughter. It's just I don't want to have to explain, or deal with them."

"We'll deal with that once we know if they're leaving today. I just want you to think about it. Now we should get up, as you said your parents will be here shortly and I want to see how Abbi's doing this morning."

"I guess I'm going to have some explaining to do anyway."

"Why?" He pulled back to look at here.

"You're going to be wearing the same closes from yesterday. Mom's going to realize it and know you stayed the night." She tried her best to shrug it off but the thought of a lecture from her mother turned her stomach.

"Don't worry, beautiful, I have a change of clothes in the truck." He slipped out of bed to stand before her, still in his jeans. "Don't give me those wide eyes again, it's not for the reason you're thinking. I don't keep extra clothes in the truck for one-night stands."

"Then why do you?"

"It's a habit I formed in Denver. Sometimes I'd leave the office to do evening rounds at the hospital and get caught up in an emergency. Being the newest doctor to the practice, the others made me handle a lot of the calls that came in during the night. Many nights I'd end up crashing in the doctor rooms at the hospital or on the sofa in my office. A change of clothes came in handy, same with fresh scrubs. If you don't mind I'll grab them and then use your shower."

She was tempted to tease him about joining him in the shower, but the idea alone sent her blood racing. Damn, she wanted this man, wanted him naked, but she barely knew him. Her mind screamed for her to slow down or she'd end up with a broken heart, while her body was raring to go. She wanted to feel his touch all over her naked body, his lips on hers, but more importantly, she wanted the intimate touches lovers share. The looks so full of heat they could melt the snow off a roof in the middle of winter. She wanted it as much as she needed her next breath.

He strolled from the room and she watched the way the jeans contoured to his butt as he walked. It took all she had not go after him, to push him back down on the bed and demand he make her feel like a woman. Her body was so full of desires she hadn't felt in so long and it scared her. She needed to get her head around what was happening between them before she let her body control the situation and she ended up naked with him.

What's wrong with me? I've known him for two short days and I'm already trying to have sex with him.

* * *

Ella stepped out of the truck in front of Winterbloom and took in the old Bed and Breakfast. In all the years since she was here the only thing that had changed was the owner. Chloe had inherited it from her grandmother, and now she owned it with her husband Jordan. They'd hired an innkeeper, Hope, since Ella's last visit. The owner's cabin was also a new addition and it gave the new family privacy. It also kept the guests from being disturbed by the newest addition to the Shepherd family, Bianca.

"You coming?" James looked back at her from the front of the truck where he was standing.

"Yes." She smiled and went to him. "I was just thinking. I knew Chloe years ago and I'm glad to see she stills owns Winterbloom. This place was her grandmother's heart and soul. Even with the change of ownership, it doesn't look like it's changed much at all."

"I wasn't here then, but I know that even with Hope, Chloe is still very hands-on. Jordan has been trying to get her to relax more, since Hope can handle the inn, but even with the baby she still finds time," James explained as they headed to the front door.

"Sounds like Chloe."

"What sounds like me?" Chloe appeared from the side of the house and as her gaze found Ella she stopped midstride. "Hell, Ella, is that you? I can't believe it."

"It's been years." Ella took her hand from his and went to the other woman, quickly wrapping her arms around Chloe, tears rolling down her face. "Too long."

"It has. Come around back to my place and let's catch up…that is unless you're busy."

"No, I have a little time. You have a guest staying here who I've come to see but he's not expecting me. Plus I want to see this baby girl I heard you had." Ella stepped back and looked at her friend. "You look great for just giving birth."

"I'm not yet back to my pre-pregnancy body, but this place and Bianca keep me hopping enough that it won't be long. My baby girl is already nine weeks, I can't believe it."

"Believe it, I saw Bianca hours after she was born." As if James had reminded them he was there, they turned to face him.

"I'm sorry." Chloe raised an eyebrow at him. "Did you come to see Jordan?"

"Actually, he's with me." She held out her hand to him, and when he took it she slid her fingers between his, interlocking them.

"Ahh, it won't be long before the gossip mill has something new to buzz about." Chloe laughed. "Come on, let's get some sweet tea and you can fill me in." She turned on her heels and headed back the way she'd come.

"Do you want me to find Gioven or Jordan so you can spend time with Chloe?" James leaned in close enough so Chloe wouldn't overhear.

"No, stay with me." She squeezed his hand, unsure what she'd managed to get herself into. It had been years since she had seen Chloe, but she thought they'd just pick up where they left off, while something in Ella warned her to be cautious. Rushing this newfound freedom that seemed almost too good to be true could be disastrous in the end.

A small part of her wished she could go back to the life she had a few days ago. She found security in the cabin, but it was also lonely. The comfort, friendship, and attraction she found in James was something she didn't want to give up, not even for the sanctuary of the woods.

James squeezed her hand, almost as if he realized she was spiraling downward with her thoughts. "I'll be there and it will be good for you to catch up with an old friend."

Chloe climbed the steps to the log cabin ranch halfway around the lake, between Winterbloom's main building and the cabins along the far side of the lake. "Who are you here to see anyway?"

"Gioven Sparks."

Chloe let the screen door bang shut without going in as she turned to them. "You can't possibly know him?"

"Umm." Ella suddenly felt unsure of herself.

"Jordan called me yesterday to help him at On the Rocks and Ella was with me. She helped us get him into the truck, even drove my truck over so I could bring Gioven's. She was able to get through to him while we couldn't," James explained, brushing his thumb over Ella's knuckles.

"I told him I'd stop by and visit with him. Why, is something wrong?"

Chloe glanced inside the door and then turned back to Ella. "You need to stay away from him. He's dangerous, especially once he's had a few drinks."

"He's sweet," she hazarded, but Chloe shook her head.

"When he's not drinking, maybe...but he can't give up the bottle. He's staying here because he's an old combat comrade of Jordan's, and I love my husband, otherwise I'd have told him to leave." Chloe crossed her arms over her chest. "I'm thankful for his service to our country, but he needs help...otherwise he is too dangerous to be around. Whatever he saw during his time in the Marines was too much for him, and the alcohol makes it worse."

"That's enough, Chloe," Jordan snapped from the other side of the door.

"I don't want her getting hurt because she doesn't understand the risks," Chloe insisted as Jordan stepped out of the house with Bianca in his arms.

"His scars might be hidden, but he's still a wounded Marine, not a freak show. I won't stand by while you criticize a man who covered my ass on missions." He handed the baby to her before continuing. "Think back to what happened when I stumbled upon your establishment during a storm."

"That's different."

"I don't think it is." Jordan nodded to the chairs on the porch. "Have a seat and let me tell you how I met Chloe."

"We don't really need to hear this," Ella said, nervousness lacing her words, but Jordan was already settling onto one of the porch rockers.

"I think you do. It will give you some insight on me but it will also allow you to understand what might be going on with Gioven." Jordan waited until everyone was seated before continuing. "A nasty storm was bearing down on Clearwater, but I didn't care, I had a personal mission and I was going to get it done. No storm was going to stand in my way, not even one that was expected to stall over the area and drop up to ten feet of snow on the town over a five day period. You might be wondering what was so important that I would risk everything for it, but I'll get to that."

"Not for some time, as your car broke down and stranded you here." Chloe smiled. "It was right after my Grandmother passed away, and I was waiting for the paperwork to go through which would allow me to reopen, so I wasn't expecting any guests. Jordan wasn't nearly as welcoming as he seems now. He was a grouchy wet man who demanded a room."

"You forgot the fact that you were threatening me with one of the logs you just carried in." Jordan smirked at Ella. "She clung to this log like she was ready to beat my head in with it."

"I was alone for the first time and there was a strange man standing in my foyer. I believe I had a right." Just like that, the tension eased from Chloe and she laughed as she bounced her daughter in her lap. "Remember the fight Ryan put up with you staying? That's when he forced Goldie, my golden retriever on me."

"We're straying from the point." Jordan reached across to lay his hand on his wife's thigh. "Like Gioven I was discharged from the Marines because of post-traumatic stress disorder. I tried to get help through the military but it didn't help. Guilt continued to eat at me, haunting me in my dreams. My first night here was no different, at least not with a dream, but I didn't say anything to Chloe and she came to me."

She adjusted the baby so she could lay her hand over his. "His screaming woke me, and not knowing what was wrong I raced to his room to help."

"When she tried to wake me, I wrapped my hand around her throat. I remember feeling her throat constrict as she fought to breathe, while Goldie barked and snapped at me." When Jordan looked at Ella the sadness and guilt from that day shined in his eyes. "I wasn't in my right mind when she woke me. So I will agree with Chloe on the fact that when Gioven drinks he isn't the same person. I know he'd never *intentionally* hurt you, but you do need to be careful."

Ella wasn't willing to back down. Maybe someone else could get him to see things as no one else had. "I understand what you're saying, but I can't just go back to my cabin and forget about him. I think we connected. I recognized something in his eyes that was familiar to me, and I can understand what he's going through to a point. I don't want to see him waste years of his life like I have."

"I was hoping you were going to say something like that. I can see the commitment in your eyes, but also because I think he needs you." Jordan nodded. "There's a little more you need to know before you visit him."

"What's that?"

"The reason I was willing to travel through that storm." Jordan leaned forward, placing his elbows on his knees. "On my last deployment I saw some shit that stuck with me, but it was the death of a good friend of mine that was my breaking point. He had a wife and a baby on the way, a child he never got to meet." He glanced over at Bianca.

"You don't have to do this." Chloe squeezed his hand.

"I know...but Gioven was there that night. The three of us went through boot camp together, we watched out for each other. It's why I invited him here. I'll help him because I won't lose him. I might have been responsible for my friend James, but I won't let it happen again."

Ella turned to James with a quizzical expression on her face, and he shrugged. "Not me."

"No." Jordan tried to smile but couldn't quite manage it. "James Ray, not your James. Confusing, but bear with me a moment until I get this out."

"Take your time," Ella said.

"I was supposed to be on that watch, but James switched with me because I was sick. He took my shift...he died in my place." Jordan took a deep breath, trying to regain his composure. "I came back a mess. I even went to the military shrink, but it didn't help. They discharged me because of it. They train you for years to fight, to kill. But when it's your best friend, a guy who's like a brother to you, the guy who went through boot camp and all the training with you, they tell you to forget about it. You can't forget it and go on like nothing happened. I was there, I should have done something more."

"Jordan..." Chloe moved to the edge of the chair before he finally looked at her. "You did everything you could. No one blames you."

Jordan moved his chair closer to his wife and baby, his arm now wrapped around Chloe's shoulders as if he was trying to ground himself in the moment. "I had no plans to let that blizzard stand in my way. I was passing through to Idaho to where James's wife lives. I promised him I would stop in and see her and the baby once I made it back to the States. I wasn't sure if I was making the right choice. I was sure she blamed me, but a promise is a promise…and I planned to keep it."

"Everything was fine in the end. Megan never blamed you, and she has a beautiful daughter, Stella." Chloe tried to lighten the tension. "They're coming to stay here for the holidays."

"Yeah." Jordan nodded before looking back at Ella. "I'm telling you this because I want you to understand what it's like when we come back from overseas. Adjustment back to normal life is complicated. I was there when James was killed, but it was nothing like that last mission Gioven was on. Even I don't know all the details, but it was a cluster-fuck."

"I'm just here to talk to him. If I can do anything to help him I will, but I'm not a therapist." Ella wasn't sure what he expected her to do but she wanted to make it clear there'd be no miracles.

"Therapists, what do they know?" His dislike for the profession was evident. "When I came back they basically told me I should just get over it, but I couldn't, I don't know how. They wanted me to talk it out, be rational—embrace the fact that people die in a war. Marines die, soldiers die, I get that. This was different. James wasn't just a Marine, he was my friend. We covered each other's asses when shit hit the fan. Even with that, he died in my place and that was the part I couldn't accept. I guess I still can't."

If he couldn't accept what happened to him at this point, how was she supposed to help Gioven accept it? From what Jordan said, it seemed like Gioven's problems didn't lie so much with the death of a friend, but with whatever had happened on that last mission. She wasn't sure she even wanted to know, but what she did want was to help him in any way she could. The look they shared at On the Rocks gave her hope that he wanted help. That was the key; otherwise, anything they tried was a waste.

Small Town Doctor

Chapter Eleven

Ella strolled hand in hand with James around the lake, heading toward Gioven's cabin, but with every step she grew unsure of the situation. Jordan had shared his past and what he went through when he left the Marines, but instead of helping her understand, it made her feel unworthy. Could she handle this?

Gioven needed help. It didn't have to be professional, as Jordan proved when he'd found Chloe, but Ella wasn't sure she was the right person. She wasn't as emotionally invested in Gioven as Chloe was with Jordan. She barely knew him, and one shared look didn't entitle her to learning his deepest, darkest secrets. She wasn't sure if Gioven would let *anyone* know those things, let alone her.

Jordan and the two other former Marines who'd begun their life in Clearwater should be able to help Gioven. They'd all witnessed combat. So why was she here trying to help him while Jordan sat back at the cabin with his new family? Where were the others?

"What's on your mind?" When she looked up at James, he added, "Your steps have slowed like you're second guessing things. Are you worried about Abbi and your parents?"

"No, I know she's fine. I was wondering where the other Marines are. Jordan mentioned the fact that two of their other combat brothers settled down here, so why aren't they trying to help him?" She paused and glanced out at the lake. "Don't they care that someone they served with is suffering?"

"Cameron White owns Clearwater Combat and Guns, which keeps him busy but he's been here. Juan Carlos Marquez has his hands full. He convinced his mother and eight younger siblings to move here, so they've settled in nicely, but he's busy with the younger siblings. Between helping Cameron with CCG while he's spending more time with Tessa, his family duties, not to mention planning a Halloween wedding, his hands are full."

"Halloween wedding?" She turned to look at him while images of the bridal party and guests in elaborate costumes danced around her thoughts.

"Rebecca is J.C.'s soon-to-be wife and she loves the fall season. So they're having the wedding in two weeks. J.C. is biting at the bit, he didn't want to wait this long, but he'd give Rebecca the moon if she wanted it. Plus, it's the least he can do since she helped convince his family to move here. It gave J.C. a new lease on life."

"Why, did he have similar problems as Jordan?""

"J.C. lost his leg when the Humvee he was riding in hit an IED. After leaving the Marines, he was at a loss as to what to do with his life. He felt like a cripple and didn't want anyone's charity. He only came to Clearwater because Cameron needed someone to help him with the shop when his daughter Rosalie was born. So, he found a new life here."

"It would seem Clearwater is a town for starting over. If we're not careful, we're going to have a whole platoon of former Marines settling down here," she joked, nodding toward the cabin. "I guess we should see if he's willing to see us."

"He wants to see you. He has an eye on you. If I don't watch out, he might try to sweep you off your feet," James teased before continuing down the path to Gioven's.

"I don't know if I ever had two men fighting for my attention, this could be fun." She leaned closer to him. "I'm just kidding. I don't know how this happened between us, but I'm happy."

One of the cabin doors opened, catching her attention, and a moment later Gioven stood in the doorframe. "Jordan called to tell me you were on your way and to make sure I was sober." His tone radiated mild annoyance. "What can I do for you?"

"I thought I'd stop by and maybe we could talk." Ella came to stand a few feet in front of him.

"I don't need pity. I was fine the other day at On the Rocks."

"That was yesterday," she clarified, as he rubbed his forehead in obvious confusion. "You were drunk, stumbling, and fighting the guys. Then I came over. I understand your suffering right now, but I want to help."

"What does she think she can do that the Marine shrink couldn't?" Gioven eyed James.

"She's trying to be a hand for you to reach out to. Someone at your side." James slid his hand along her back.

"Guys, I'm standing right here, so please don't talk as if I'm not." She crossed her arms over her chest. "Either you want to talk to me, or you want to be left alone. I've come all this way and I'm not standing out here in this cool air while you figure it out. So what's it going to be?"

"Unless you've brought a drink, maybe you should carry on your way." Gioven's large frame was imposing, but he didn't frighten her in the least.

"No drink, and you don't need it." She turned to James. "Forget it. He obviously doesn't want to see us. I should know better than anyone…if a recluse isn't ready to deal with the real world, you can't force it on them. It's the same with someone who's choosing the bottle over facing up to life."

"What do you know about it?" Gioven pushed off the doorframe to stand straight. "Woman, you've stayed here safe and sound while I was overseas seeing shit you couldn't even conjure in your nightmares."

"You might be right, but I have an idea." She took a deep breath of the cool air and pushed forward. "I have a daughter, Abbi, she's four years old now."

"What does this have to do with anything?"

"Just stand there and listen to her, you might learn something from it." James laid a hand on her shoulder. "Go ahead."

"As I was saying, my daughter…" Now that she'd been interrupted, she wasn't sure what to say.

"Go ahead, Ella, you're doing fine."

"I don't know how to put this. Besides telling James, I've never told anyone my story." She took a few deep breaths as James rubbed her shoulder. "Abbi's father, Josh, murdered a man and seriously wounded two others. When I tried to stop him from taking a bar fight outside, he pushed me back, slamming me into the corner of the bar. I lay on the floor unconscious while he shot someone. Then as I watched he slammed a man's head into the pavement over and over until there was nothing left but blood and gore."

"What does this have to do with anything?" Gioven asked.

"I'm telling you this because you need to realize you're not the only one who has things that haunt them. Instead of facing it, I hid away in my grandparents' cabin, trying to forget it. It haunted me every moment. My nightmares were filled with it happening over and over again. I believed everyone blamed me because Josh wasn't a local, he was there visiting me. I thought they'd take their hatred for what happened that night out on my innocent daughter. So I hid, refusing to come into town."

"What changed?"

"Abbi got sick. I was scared out of my mind because she wouldn't eat or drink, her fever was high. I was alone on the mountain with no phone, no car, and essentially no way to get her the help she needed. The Sheriff, Ryan, he'd stop at the cabin every so often just to check to make sure I was all right. I guess he felt somewhat responsible for me living there since he's the one who took Josh into custody. The point is, Abbi's health was my wake-up call. It also brought James into my life."

"Well, I don't have a child I need to worry about." Gioven stepped back, his hand on the door like he was going to shut it on them.

"What about all the children, town residents, and everyone else you'd have risked yesterday by getting behind the wheel drunk?" James placed his hand on the door, making it hard for Gioven to shut it. "Do you want to be responsible for someone's death because you drove drunk?"

"I don't have to worry about that, Jordan took my keys. I'm not going anywhere. Now if you'd leave, there's a bottle inside with my name on it." He glared at them, then slammed the door in their faces.

"Gioven!" she shouted at the closed door.

"Come on, sweetie, he's not ready." James wrapped his arm around her waist and practically carried her away from the door. "There's nothing you can do until he's willing to accept that he has to move past what happened overseas. He might have left his fallen brothers behind, but he's still got a life he's meant to live."

"How am I supposed to just do nothing?"

"The same way your parents did."

"What?" She dug her heels into the ground, refusing to move another step.

"When you moved into the cabin, your parents left you be. You said it yourself, they didn't completely understand your reasoning but they didn't fight you. They visited every month or so but it wasn't until after Abbi was born that Bea started pushing you to move. You weren't ready to leave the cabin until recently, just like he's not ready."

"You're saying I'm supposed to stand by and do nothing?"

"What you're feeling now, that utter helplessness, that's what your parents dealt with." He smirked and pulled her close. "It's not easy, but yes. You can visit, but like today he might not want to see you. Sometimes he might not even open the door, while other times he might invite you in and the two of you could spend hours talking. You have to give him time. Eventually, I believe we can get him to see what he's doing to himself."

"Right now the bottle is his escape as the cabin was mine." She glanced back at the cabin one last time before they continued around the lake and back to James's truck.

She had a newfound respect for her parents and what they must have gone through all those years. She had thought being holed up in cabin only affected her, but even though her parents weren't there it affected them as well.

I think it's time to move on…from the cabin and everything. Time to live life again and maybe more.

* * *

The day had been a little bumpier than James had hoped, and he wasn't completely sure how the visit with Gioven impacted Ella, as she remained a little too quiet throughout most of the day. Now he sat in Abbi's room reading her a story so Ella and her parents could talk. His nerves were on edge. When Ella had asked him to read the story, she had mentioned she needed time to talk to her parents before they left, but he was clueless as to what it involved. Was she thinking about moving to Cheyenne?

He should've been joyful that she was willing to venture back into town, but the thought of her leaving Clearwater sent a ping of regret through him. They'd just started to get to know each other, and he didn't want her to go. In a short period of time, Ella had grown to mean a lot to him, and Abbi was already in his heart. A little family he didn't know he wanted had almost become his entire world.

"Is Mommy mad at Grammy?"

He set the book aside and looked over at Abbi who was laying beside him on the bed. "No sweetie. Why do you ask?"

"I heard her yelling at Grammy last night after you brought me to bed."

"You were supposed to be sleeping. If you were awake why didn't you say something?"

"I wasn't. I was so tired, but they woke me. Grammy wants to take me away but I don't want to go without Mommy." She cuddled Mr. Bear closed to her chest and tears glistened in her eyes.

"You're not going anywhere, sweetie." James wrapped his arm around her shoulder. "Grammy thought you were sick he wanted to take you to the doctor."

"But *you're* my doctor." She laid her head on his chest, Mr. Bear squished between them. "Aren't you?"

"That I am, but Grammy didn't know that. She came a long way to see you when she thought you were sick, and to get you the help she thought you needed, so don't be mad at her."

"Then she won't take me away?"

"No, you're going to stay right here with your mom." With the tips of his fingers, he brushed her blonde hair away from her face.

"With you too? Or are you leaving now that I'm feeling better?"

"With your mom's permission, I'm hoping to see a lot more of the two of you." He kissed the top of her head. "Now, you need to rest so you can get all better."

The bedroom door swung open and Ella stood there. "He's right. You need sleep. Why don't you take a short nap? James and I will just be in the other room if you need us."

He raised his eyebrow at her in question as he slipped off the bed and covered Abbi with her blanket. "Sleep, and maybe we can do something special when you wake up."

When he stepped out of Abbi's bedroom and back into the living room, he noticed her parents had gone. He pulled the door shut and turned to Ella. "Where's Bea and Dale?"

"They made some excuse about needing to go to Jackson Hole before they left. They'll be back in an hour or two to say goodbye, and then they're hitting the road for Cheyenne. Dad prefers night driving anyway, so this works better for them."

"Does that mean you'll come and spend the night at my place tonight?" He moved farther into the living room and kept his voice low so as not to disturb Abbi.

"I don't know." She sank down onto the sofa and pulled her legs up against her chest. "Going into town for a visit or a drive is one thing, but this is another. What is Abbi going to think if I'm shacking up with her doctor?"

"That you have good taste?" He joked before sitting beside her. "Would it make a difference if I wasn't her doctor? Michael could take over her care."

"No!" She hugged her legs tighter to her chest. "I trust you. I know it sounds crazy, but I do."

"Then trust me enough to know you'll be safe at my house. It's far enough from downtown and off the beaten track that no one will stumble upon you. You'll have the privacy you have here, but you'll be close to me."

"James, I don't even know what's happening between us."

He laid a hand on her knee. "What do you want to be happening?"

"What's that supposed to mean?"

"Do you believe in love at first sight?" When her eyes widened, he ran his hand down her leg. "I didn't think I did before. As a doctor I believed it was all a chemical change that would eventually wear off. You might find someone attractive but love had to be developed, built, it wasn't something that just happened. Now…well, I believe."

"Why?"

"When I got out of the truck and you were busy giving Ryan a piece of your mind, I couldn't help but stare. You're beautiful. The more time I spend with you the more I know I want you by my side." He squeezed her thigh, gently but with enough pressure that she felt it. "I didn't want to tell you any of this because you have other things on your mind right now. The stress of leaving the cabin for the first time in years, Abbi's health, not to mention your parents."

"Then why did you?"

"Because you need to know where I stand. I'd rather have you by my side than anything else in the world. I understand you might not know how you feel, and this might be too much, but don't discount what's happening between us because you're scared." He didn't want to rush her, and had planned to keep his desires to himself, but she'd asked and she deserved to know. He wasn't expecting anything from her, but damn did he want her to say she felt the same way.

This is the woman I want to spend the rest of my life with. Now…if I can only convince her.

Small Town Doctor

Chapter Twelve

Against Ella's better judgment, she sent James home alone, claiming she needed time to think things through. She hadn't wanted to lead him on until she was sure she was willing to risk her heart again. It wasn't just her she had to think about; she also had to consider her daughter. Abbi had already begun to latch on to James, and Ella didn't want her heart broken if he disappeared.

She sat there staring at the keys her parents had left on her table before they'd started the journey back to Cheyenne. They'd made the excuse to go to Jackson Hole to get a rental car so they could leave their SUV for her to use. This way she could go into town, or visit James as she pleased. It was the first step in regaining her life, her independence. She could use the SUV until she purchased one to replace the one she'd sold years ago when she moved to the cabin.

Part of her wanted to load Abbi into the SUV and drive into town. She needed to see James, to tell him she realized what she wanted. She wanted him, what they had, and all the things they *could* have. She wanted to go to Clearwater's Halloween festival, to the Halloween party at his sister's house, but more importantly, she wanted to do it with him. To be with him in a way she hadn't yet experienced. It wasn't about sex. It was the intimacy of his touch, the embraces, the way he made her feel. She wanted it all, and so much more.

Abbi played quietly in front of the fire, one of her favorite movies on the television, while Ella palmed the keys and let them fall back onto the table. To go or not to go was what she was trying to decide when she heard a truck coming up the drive.

James?

No, it couldn't be. He said he had to work, which mean it had to be Ryan. The one person she really didn't want to deal with.

"Abs, I've got to step outside for a moment." She dropped the keys back on the table and hoped to cut Ryan off before he even got out of the vehicle. He might have only been checking in to see how Abbi was doing, but Ella had too much on her mind to be sociable.

Stepping outside she was surprised to see James instead. He'd been on her thoughts since he'd left, and now there he was stepping out of his truck in his perfectly pressed shirt and tie, his slacks sporting a perfect crease. It was so different from the way he had looked when he first arrived to help Abbi.

"I couldn't stop thinking about you, so I got Michael to cover for me for a bit and I thought we could have lunch." He held up a brown paper sack. "It's not much, sandwiches from Express Ohh's, but it's what I could do quickly."

"It's better than what I was going to make. Macaroni and Cheese because it's Abbi's favorite, but not that boxed crap. The real stuff with the longhorn cheese that melts perfectly over all the noodles so that every bite makes you think you're in Heaven."

"Hmm, I can't say I've experienced that."

When he came to stand in front of her, she wrapped her arms around his neck. "How about I cook it for you tomorrow at your place and you can experience the wonders of it?"

"Sounds wonderful. I can come back up this evening to get you, after I finish up at the office." He tipped his head toward the SUV. "You're parents still here? I thought they'd be gone, so I didn't get extra sandwiches, but I can run back into town."

"No, they left last night. The SUV is so I can come and go as I please. So how about I meet you downtown tonight? I mean, if your offer of us staying at your place still stands. We can watch some movies until Abbi goes to bed and then I'm sure we can find something to fill our time. This way we can be together and you can be close to the hospital in case you're needed. Then tomorrow I'll make the macaroni and cheese for us."

He wrapped his arms around her waist, pulling her tight. "That sounds perfect. Let's go inside and eat because there's a certain little girl I brought a special treat for."

"Wait." She took hold of his hand as he tried to slip past her and into the house. "I need to tell you something."

"Ella, is something wrong?"

"Just the opposite." She smirked. "Last night I realized I love you." She caught the spark of desire in his eyes when she spoke. "You're all I've thought about since you showed up here in your jeans and that plum dress shirt with the top buttons undone. You're different, and I love that about you. How Michael ever offered you a partnership when you're so different than him is beyond me…but I'm grateful for it, because it brought you here."

He kissed her gently on the lips. "We met in medical school and were inseparable until he decided he wanted to practice here. Then Jes agreed to be Michael and his ex-wife's surrogate. When we arrived a few weeks before Christmas, she found Michael alone. Peg had divorced him and was engaged to someone else, living in Denver. Long story short, when I came up to spend the holidays with them he offered me the position so he could spend more time with Jes and my nieces. It worked out nicely as it let me move closer and have an active role as Uncle James to Kari and Kami."

"Then you found me and Abbi," she said, feeling her cheeks flush.

"That I did." He laced his fingers through hers. "Maybe next weekend you'll allow me to take you and Abbi to the festival at the lake. I think Abbi would love it."

"I know she would. She's been asking where you were and if you were coming back all morning. It seems my little girl has taken to you." She swallowed the fear that was rising within her as they made their way into the house.

"James, you came back!" Abbi tossed her doll aside and ran toward them.

"Did you think I wouldn't come back to you? You're my little munchkin and I brought you something special. Come sit at the table and you can have it."

"What is it?" She bounced up and down with excitement.

"Sit down and James will give it to you." Ella eyed her daughter as she grabbed drinks, while he sat down with Abbi and began to dig into the paper bag.

"Now, what I'm about to pull out of this bag you can't have until after you eat the sandwich I brought you. Understand?" Abbi nodded and he pulled out a large frosted brownie. "The owner of Express Ohh's, Jennifer, ensures me this is the best chocolate brownie you will ever eat."

"Yum!" She reached for it just as Ella sat the drinks on the table.

"Oh, no you don't. You must eat your sandwich first or James and I will enjoy the brownie without you," Ella reminded her.

With a reluctant nod, Abbi took the sandwich James proffered. "Will you stay and watch a movie with me?"

"I'm sorry, sweetie, I have to go back to work." He unwrapped his own sandwich and took a bite.

"Tonight." Ella sat down on the other side of him. "We're going to have a sleepover at his house tonight. We'll watch movies and have popcorn."

"Why can't we do it here?"

"He's on call with the hospital and needs to be close to town. Maybe we can go to Happy Ever After and get some new books. Or some ice cream. How does that sound?"

"Okay." She nodded eagerly as she ate.

"I'm excited to have you both here tonight. How about we treat ourselves? Before the popcorn, we can order pizza." He grinned as Abbi's eyes widened. "I'll take that as a yes."

They made small talk as they finished their lunch, but to her it didn't matter what they talked about just that they were together. After all those years alone, she was glad to have his company, and to feel the love blossoming within her.

* * *

The day had come to end, though not as quickly as James would have liked. Knowing Ella and Abbi were waiting for him had given him something to look forward to, and it also seemed to make the day drag along. If it hadn't been for an emergency appointment after one of the Bragger boys broke his arm after falling from his bike, he'd have been off earlier. In a small town like this, parents liked when their family doctor stopped into the emergency room to look at the x-ray and ensure them their child would be fine. He had done that, and it calmed Mrs. Bragger when she knew her son's arm would heal in a matter of weeks without surgery. Little moments like that were why he enjoyed his work.

Tonight, he knew he'd be enjoying it a lot more. Stepping into the parking lot, he found Ella's SUV parked next to his truck, waiting. He couldn't keep the corners of his lips from turning up into a smile as he neared them. This was happiness, something he hadn't thought he'd find. Heck, he hadn't even been looking for it. Until they'd come into his life, he had been content with being single and his work.

"Hey, handsome." Ella stepped out of the SUV. "Abbi hasn't stopped talking about our pizza and movie date all afternoon. I'm not sure if she's more excited for Tony's Pizza or for your company. She's dying for you to read her another bedtime story, because according to her, you do it better than I ever did."

"She did mention that, something about the voices." He wrapped his arm around her back and brought her close to him. "I'll be sure to live up to the reputation."

She wrapped her arms around his neck. "I had no idea how much she had bonded with you until today. If you disappear, she's going to be heartbroken."

"What about her mother, wouldn't she be heartbroken too?" He leaned down, pressing their foreheads together. "I'm not going anywhere. I love you, beautiful."

"I love you, too."

Those three little words meant so much to him because he knew what it took for them to get there. It had taken a lot for Ella to trust him, or anyone. That was an accomplishment all in itself. *Damn, this woman is amazing and she's all mine.*

"To answer your question, yes, I'd be heartbroken if you didn't stick around." She rubbed her hand up his chest. "Maybe tonight after we get Abbi to bed we can have an adults-only evening."

He thought he knew what she meant but wasn't completely sure how far she'd let him take things. Only time would tell, and he was eager to find out. Thoughts of getting her naked ran through his mind until he wanted to take her right there. If only his co-workers, patients, and Abbi weren't watching, he just might have. This woman sent his blood rushing, and his hands itched with the urge to touch her.

Small Town Doctor

Chapter Thirteen

James had expected an adjustment period with Ella and Abbi being at his house, but the evening had gone perfectly. Pizza and movies with popcorn thrown into the mix had been a big hit with Abbi, while her favorite films played on his big screen television and the adults cuddled on the sofa. Now that Abbi was tucked into one of the guest rooms for the night, he had Ella all to himself.

He strolled into the living room, standing in the archway and watching as she put the popcorn bowls into the dishwasher. "Don't worry about those, I'll get them."

"It's the least I could do while you read her bedtime story."

He came up behind her and wrapped his arms around her waist. "Now that I'm back I can think of a better way to spend the evening."

"What did you have in mind? A physical examination?" she joked as he pressed himself against her body, his hardened shaft firm against her.

"An exam, hmm." He ran his hand down her arm until he could take her hand into his. "Come, let me show you."

"Promises, promises."

"Tonight there's no promises, just actuality." He led her back to the living room, around the furniture, to the blankets and pillows Abbi had scattered in front of the television. The fireplace crackled, sending sparks up the chimney, creating a romantic feeling now that they were alone. "Lie down."

She did as he asked, leaning back against the pillows that were pushed against the base of the sofa, and he came to sit beside her. "You know I've been looking forward to having you all to myself."

"I'm still waiting for you to show me what you had in mind." She reached out with her free hand and cupped his cheek, caressing over his stubble, along his jawline before rubbing her thumb along his chin.

"I don't want to rush you," he whispered, nuzzling against her hand.

* * *

She took a deep breath and pushed her fears aside. No longer would she deny her body what it craved, not when her future was beginning to have a new ray of hope sparkling through it.

"I want you." She continued to touch him; she couldn't stop. "Take my mind off everything else, relieve this burning desire within me and make me feel like a woman again, not just a mother. I want to feel desirable." She smirked and left out a light laugh. "This is so unlike me."

"Let me show you how desirable you are." He scooted as close to her hip as he could get and slipped his fingers into her hair. "You're beautiful."

She could feel her cheeks heat with embarrassment but before she could say anything, he closed the distance between them, claiming her lips. Immediately the saltiness from the buttered popcorn hit her. Wanting more of him, she let her tongue slip into his mouth and explore. Their tongues danced together as he moved his fingers under the hem of her sweater, gently pulling it up. When he'd tugged it as far as he could, he broke the kiss and pulled it over her head.

The warmth from the fireplace surrounded her as he tossed the shirt aside. She started to pull his off of him, but he stopped her.

"Are you sure?"

"As sure as I've ever been about anything." She stroked her fingers over his smooth stomach. "But maybe we should go to your bedroom. I'd hate for Abbi to wake up, want a drink, and stumble upon us *naked*."

"You're right, the bed would be better." He stood and scooped her into his arms.

"I can walk."

"Oh, beautiful, I've seen you do that and the sway of your hips can send a grown man to his knees."

She chuckled and leaned her head against his chest, letting him carry her down the hall to the master bedroom. The walk seemed longer than it had earlier when he'd showed her the area and had taken their bags down to their rooms. She wrapped her arms around his neck. "So, the sway of my hips turn you on, eh?"

"One of many things." They entered the large bedroom, and he kicked the door shut behind them, heading straight to the large bed with the black leather headboard. He laid her in the center on the warm blue comforter.

He wasted no time stripping off his clothes and she suspected he was also overcome by yearning. She tried to memorize the sight of him naked before he crawled onto the bed next to her and went to work on the buttons of her jeans.

She stared at him while her hand slid down his chest until she found his shaft. She wrapped her fingers around it and rubbed down the length, painstakingly slow. She teased her fingernails along his girth, just enough that he could feel it without causing pain. "I love when you look at me like that."

"Like what?" His voice hitched up a notch.

"Like I complete you. Like I'm the woman you've looked for all your life."

"You are." At those two simple words, her grip on his shaft loosened and he was able to slip away.

"Get back here," she ordered, unable to keep the smirk off her face.

"Later, now unhook your bra. I want to see all of you. Naked and waiting for me. Oh, what a beautiful sight that will be."

Not seeing herself as he did, she wanted to deny it. Josh had made sure he tore her self-esteem to shreds before they parted ways. She might have had the skinny body many women strived for, but that was from hard work. Thoughts of her appearance were pushed away when he claimed her mouth. She moaned around his unrelenting kiss.

When the kiss final ended, leaving her breathless, he whispered, "If you won't take it off, I'll work around it." He pushed her bra to the side as he feverishly claimed her nipple with his lips, while he reached with his other hand to the waistband of her jeans and pushed them down her legs. With them went her last shred of reservation.

"Please…" She reached out, her hand landing firmly on his chest, forcing him closer to her. His shaft pressed tight against her thigh. In his arms for the first time, she felt safe and wanted. Her nails ran over chest, her need riding her.

His fingers slipped between her legs, stoking the fire within her until he was dragging pleasure from her in hard, hot waves. He thrust his fingers into her as he continued to wring more pleasure from her core with his thumb.

"I need you inside me. Please…"

He slipped his hand away and moved to hover over her, angled between her spread thighs, then he glided his shaft over her opening, coaxing a moan from her. Slowly he glided the length in, just a little at first as he worked his way inside her tight passage. Halfway in he stopped and slid out, even as she clung to him trying to force him to stay. Once he was out, he gripped her hips and slammed his length into her, filling her completely. Rocking their bodies back and forth, each thrust gained momentum. He gave her no time to catch her breath.

She leaned back, grabbing the edge of the headboard, her body arched toward him. With every thrust, her breasts bounced with appreciation, calling to him. Without losing his rhythm, he dipped his head and drew his tongue along each nipple, blowing gently on them.

"Faster." She lifted her hips to meet his as he pumped into her.

"So demanding." With each stroke he brought it up another level, slowly intensifying the tempo until she was ready to roll him over and do it herself. When her control was almost at its limit, his hips slammed into her as she met each thrust.

"Come for me, Ella. I want to feel your muscles tighten against me."

Minutes later, an orgasm coursed through her. Her body arched into him, nails digging into the soft skin of his back.

Seconds later he buried his head in her shoulder, growling her name as his own release followed. Kissing her neck, he stayed buried deep within her. "I love you, Ella Carmichael." He kissed a line along her neck, working his way to her ear.

"If you keep doing that, I'm going to be ready for round two."

As if agreeing, his shaft twitched, hardening against the walls of her core. "I think we can arrange that."

"Umm." She moaned, teasing her fingers along his sides. "You might be Doctor Eveready, but I do need a little recovery time."

He slipped off her to cuddle next to her as their breathing began to return to normal. In his embrace she was content, safe, but most importantly she'd found love. Everything was perfect. It was more than she could have asked for. He was amazing with her daughter and he loved her. *Love*. Her heart fluttered until she thought it would fly away.

"Ella…"

She turned her head just enough to look at him. "What's wrong?"

"Stay with me."

"I told Abbi we'd spend the night here. Remember I'm making macaroni and cheese tomorrow."

He tucked a strand of her hair behind her ear. "No, stay here permanently."

"What?"

"Dale mentioned that the place your grandfather had before he built the cabin you're living in has a bigger plot of land. It's closer to town, and I checked…there's cell reception in the area."

She leaned on her elbow to look at him. "I don't understand. That cabin has been unlivable for years. What does it have to do with anything?"

"I want you to stay here while we build a house on that land. I want to be with you but your cabin doesn't make that easy without the cell reception. We can start what we need to do tomorrow and if we hurry maybe they can break ground for the house before winter. If we get a large team working we might be able to get started before winter freezes the ground and puts off building a house until spring." He teased his index finger along the curve of her jaw. "I want you to marry me, so we can build a life together with Abbi."

"Marry…" She leaned back from him and tried to remember to breathe. She couldn't believe what he'd said. He wanted her to leave her sanctuary, to be thrown back into Clearwater life full-force, but also to marry him. Was he asking too much? Marriage to a doctor— she had an idea what that meant. She couldn't have the private life she wanted, not in Clearwater. He'd always have to be in town, he'd be on call day and night.

His career hadn't been an issue until that moment when she realized that he'd be a center point in Clearwater. He'd have to be a part of the town, events, and so much more. She wasn't sure she was ready for that. That didn't even included the fact there were hospital functions he'd have to attend, the biggest being the hospital's Christmas party.

She loved him, but she wasn't sure she would ever be the woman he needed for his career. Could she be a socialite so she could have love? She wasn't sure, especially if she had to be surrounded by people in social functions again. What if they mentioned her past? It wouldn't let her go, wouldn't let her have a life again—or love.

"Whoa, Ella. I can see the fear in your eyes." He pulled her close to her. "Fine, we don't have to discuss marriage right now. Just stay here with me. We'll take it one day at a time and go from there."

"James, I love you."

"Why do I feel like there's a *but* coming?"

"Oh, James!" She ran her hand over his chest. "Have you thought maybe I'm not the woman for you?"

"Why would you say that?"

"I'll never be a socialite and that's what you need. You need someone who can be on your arm for the hospital parties, to attend town events with you. I'm not sure I'm that person. Your social life will be rich because of your position but I'm not sure I can handle that."

"You've done fine with everything so far. What about going to Winterbloom the other day? You glowed while we visited with Chloe and her friends. That's what matters, not parties." He rubbed his hand over her back. "I'd give it all up for you and Abbi, but there's no reason we can't have everything we both want. We'll build a house where we can have the privacy you want and I can still be reached if there's an emergency."

"I don't know."

"I do," he assured her. "You're the only woman I want. Building a house on the other property will give us a place outside of town. While it's being built we can divide our time between here and your cabin. When we're there I'll have Michael cover emergencies and maybe Ryan has an extra one of those radios I can keep as back-up. There aren't many emergencies here in Clearwater, but when they do happen, Michael might need help."

"Okay, let's build the house."

He raised an eyebrow at her. "Does that mean you'll marry me?"

"I thought you said we could take this one day at a time? The house will be common ground where we can both have what we want. It will allow me to be with you, and that's what I want. Marriage…well, that's a big step. Can I think about it? I still think I'm not the right person. After years of being on my own, I'm not sure how much I can stand being around people."

"Okay. Michael and Jessi's Halloween party is just around the corner, that will give you an idea of what you're getting into. It will also prove you're going to be amazing."

"Damn, I forgot about that party." She leaned back against the pillows.

"It's going to be fine. We'll go shop for Halloween costumes for all of us and we're going to have fun."

She snuggled against him, trying to absorb his confidence, while the idea of marriage played through her mind. For a brief moment she wished she could have met James before Josh had come into her life and destroyed her.

No, she couldn't blame him for everything.

She had been the one who chose to cabin, away from everyone and everything. If she'd met James years ago, she wouldn't have had any hesitation when it came to marriage. Years ago, that was what she'd wanted, marriage and children.

But meeting Josh had brought her one thing should wouldn't change, not in a million years—Abbi.

Her daughter was the best thing that happened to her because of that union.

Everything happens for a reason.

Chapter Fourteen

The days flew by in a blur, and each day Ella and Abbi got used to their new life. Living in James's rental house held some unusual surprises; the biggest was the change in her daughter. Each day held new delights as they crept closer to Halloween and the party. Marriage still weighed heavy on her mind, and each day she gave it a stronger consideration.

"Mommy! Someone's coming up the drive." Abbi called out from the window seat where she was playing with the new baby doll James had brought home the evening before.

She forced herself to swallow the lump that was forming in her throat and look out the window. She had hoped to see James's truck approaching, but it wasn't him. A bright red SUV came to a stop near the front door.

"Sweetie, I've got your lunch on the table," Ella said absently. "Go eat and take your medication that's sitting in the cup by your drink. I'm going to see who's here."

"Can't I come?"

"No." She tried to keep the fear out of her voice. "Go eat your lunch and I'll let you have a cookie when I'm done."

With that Abbi jumped off the window seat and dashed toward the kitchen. Now that she was feeling better, her energy level had returned with a vengeance, keeping Ella on her toes. With her daughter safely out of the way, she went to the door to face this unannounced visitor. She opened the door just as a woman stepped out of the SUV.

"You must be Ella." The woman's blonde hair was pulled up into a messy clip. "From the way you're looking at me I'm assuming James didn't manage to give you a call. I'm Jessi, his sister."

"Umm, no, he didn't call."

"He was dealing with a sick child who vomited on him when I called so I'm not completely surprised that he wanted to change before he called. I guess my lead foot got here too soon."

Ella rubbed her arms trying to chance the chill around. "It's cold so why don't you come in and tell me why you're here."

"Mommy, phone." Abbi called from the doorway holding the phone out.

Ella took the phone and checked the screen, sure enough it was James. "Thank you, sweetie. Now go back inside and eat." She hit the talk button and brought the phone to her ear. "Do you have something to tell me?"

"That damn sister of mine made it there already, didn't she?"

"Yes." She smirked at Jessi and she was surprised to find she wasn't upset at all. Actually, it was kind of nice to finally meet his sister. "So she can fill me in, and you can get back to your appointments. I'll see you when you get home."

"I'm sorry, hon."

"There's no need to be. I love you."

"Love you too. Also, I'll be home early, only two appointments left unless something comes up." With that he ended the call and got back to his day.

She shut the phone off and gestured to the open door. "So, come on in. I was just feeding Abbi. Can I offer you something?"

"Just your refrigerator." Jessi opened the passenger door. "Ours died, but I've got all this food for the party tomorrow night. Our housekeeper Betty is watching the girls while I see if I can get this stuff somewhere cold. I'm meeting Michael and we're going to get a new one, hopefully we can get it delivered it tonight. Any chance you'd let me put this stuff in your refrigerator? I'll do my best to get it out of here tonight."

"Sure. We can make room." She shoved the phone in her pocket and crossed over to grab what she could from the SUV.

"Thank you. I'd have hated to waste all this food." Jessi gathered a load. "Not the best way to meet, but I'm glad to finally meet you. I've been asking James to bring you up for dinner."

"Funny, I mentioned you should come for dinner a few times but he said you were busy with the twins and getting ready for the party."

Jessi let out a laugh as they carried the food inside. "I think that brother of mine has been trying to keep you all to himself. Not that I blame him. What I can gather from my tightlipped brother, it sounds like he's in love. There's a happiness in his voice I don't think I've ever heard before."

"I think we make each other happy. I love him."

"Good. He might be my big brother, but I can be a little protective. He works hard and deserves to have someone who loves him to come home to at the end of the day."

They made small talk as they filled the refrigerator with party food, quickly hitting it off, which was something Ella had worried about. She'd been concerned that Jessi wouldn't think she was good enough for her brother. She didn't think she had to worry about it any longer.

With the last of the food put away, Ella leaned against the counter. "I don't think you have enough food," she joked as she took a long drink of the coffee she had poured while she was making Abbi's lunch.

"That's only about half of it. There are things coming from Express Ohh's tomorrow and more that doesn't have to be cold." Jessi shoved her hands into the front pockets of her jeans. "Hey there's nothing worse than running out of food. Plus, Betty goes crazy when we throw get-togethers and end up with too much food."

"I think you could feed every resident and still have leftovers."

"Is your Mom always so negative?" Jessi plopped down on the chair next to Abbi.

"Not really." Abbi chewed the last bite of her lunch. "Cookie?"

"Go ahead." Ella nodded to the tray of freshly baked chocolate chip cookies. "Jessi, want one?"

"Thanks, but I've got to get on the road. I'll call and let you know when I'll be by to grab the food. Thank you for this."

"No problem. Plus, it's James's house, I couldn't tell you no." She walked through the house toward the front door.

"Oh, I think you could have done anything you wanted. James is head over heels in love with you." She pulled open the front door. "I'm glad he's found someone like you and I look forward to getting to know you better."

"How about dinner sometime next week? I know Abbi's excited to meet the twins."

"Sounds like a plan. I hear both of our men are knocking off early today so enjoy your time with James. Once the party is out of the way we'll do lunch too, just us girls." Jessi stepped outside and the wild rushed around them. "It won't be long before winter has reclaimed its hold on this town."

Ella took a deep breath of the cold air and nodded. She loved winter, and this year she was looking forward to snuggling with James on the sofa, sharing afternoons of hot chocolate chats with Abbi, and building snowmen.

This year is going to be a season of new beginnings for all of us.

* * *

Halloween was Saturday and it seemed like every child under ten was sick and had been into James's office. Each parent had asked for the strongest antibiotics so their son or daughter would be well enough to attend the Halloween activities the town put on every year and of course to trick-or-treat. He had done his best, but it seemed like cold and flu season started earlier this year, and some children would be missing out on all the fun.

Though he knew one little girl he would personally make sure had the best Halloween ever. Abbi had never experienced the joys of trick-

or-treating, bobbing for apples, carving the pumpkin, and his favorite…eating the pumpkin seeds. He was looking forward to the holiday activities with Ella and Abbi. Christmas also promised to be quite joyful as Abbi experienced all the first time joys of that season.

Parents got to experience this during the first year of the child's life, even the second, but Abbi was older now and could experience them with a whole different excitement. He felt like a first time parent and couldn't wait to show Abbi all the things he'd enjoyed growing up. There was only one thing missing—a wedding. It would make this complete, and would give them both his last name. With a few legalities out of the way, he could officially adopt Abbi.

"We've been expecting you." Ella stood next to the bar in the kitchen, her arms crossed over her chest.

"Will you come play with me?" Abbi's head popped over the top of the sofa to look at him.

"He just got home from work, Abbi. Leave him be for a bit."

"It seems like I have to make something up to your Mom, then let me change and I'm all yours until dinner. Okay?" He placed his shoulder bag with his laptop and other paperwork he'd try to get to this weekend and went to Ella. "I'm sorry I—"

"There's no need, Jessi explained it. She called when you needed to change after an accident with a patient. I wouldn't have wanted you to wallow in it just to call me. It was just a surprise when her red SUV came pulling up the drive."

"Jessi drives too fast, always has, so I should have known she'd get here before I could call. I could have had Tonya call."

"You can't have your office manager making personal calls for you." Ella shook her head. "Plus there was nothing to worry about, Jessi is great. She's only looking out for her big brother."

"It's my job to watch over her. Well, maybe not so much now that she's married but it's hard to give up that role even if she is too old for her brother's concern."

"You're never too old and that's what family is all about. Being a pain in the…" She glanced at Abbi who seemed to be playing and ignoring them before whispering, "*Ass.* Something about love, or some other crap. Which you and Jessi have in spades. I guess if I'm honest, I'm a little jealous of that. I always wanted a sibling. Heck, I wanted to give Abbi a few brothers and sisters."

He wrapped his arms around her waist and pulled her against him. "There's no reason we can't. To be a pediatrician you have to love kids, I think I've shown that with Abbi. We could have our own." A fear crossed through her eyes, sending a tremor down her body that he tried to soothe away by rubbing his hand up her back. "If you're worried that I'd treat our own child differently than I do Abbi, then maybe you don't know me as well as I thought we knew each other."

"I didn't think that."

"Then what?" He pulled back enough to get a better look at her.

"When I gave birth to Abbi there were some complications. To make matters worse I did it in the cabin and had nearly delivered before Doctor Bowmen arrived. He wanted me to come into the office for a follow-up after the birth, but I never did. I had Abbi, Josh's trial was about to begin, I just couldn't do it. So I'm not sure if I can have any more children. It's possible the complications have made that harder or impossible."

"There's only one way to tell. We can make an appointment with Doctor Bowmen. I'll go with you if you want. Jes can watch Abbi."

"It's another reason I said I thought you deserve someone else." She looked back at Abbi and nodded. "Call him and see when he can get me in. Children are something important to me, to us, and I think it's time to find out."

"I want you to know that no matter what you find out, I love you. We have Abbi and can adopt if we want. There's always the option of a surrogate. I want you and Abbi. I won't let something like not being able to have other children stand in our way." He kissed her forehead.

"A surrogate?"

"Ah, I forgot you missed that bit of town drama."

"What do you mean? You've been here less than a year, how much town drama could you have seen during that time?"

He smirked. "I was a part of it, so was Jes. You might have known Michael was married before my sister."

"Yeah. Pat or someone."

"Peg. They couldn't have children so they wanted a surrogate. Jes volunteered. She knew Michael and always had a thing for him, but I guess from what I'm told, I was one of the reasons things never happened between them. I'm getting away from the point. Jes arrived in Clearwater a few weeks before Christmas last year, as part of the agreement. Michael and Peg had come to Denver to attend the prenatal doctor appointments and Doctor Bowmen was going to deliver them here. When she arrived to spend the last portion of her pregnancy with them, she found Michael a mess and in the process of a divorce."

"What did she do?"

"Just like she's always done when things went wrong. She put the pieces back together. Only there was a new piece to Michael's puzzle now. Somehow, in the middle of getting everything ready for the twins, because he hadn't begun the nursery or anything. Not to mention the surprise second baby that didn't announce herself until she came here and Doctor Bowmen did an ultrasound, they fell in love. There had been something between them for years, but Michael denied it because of me and medical school. This was what they needed to get together."

"An amazing love story."

"I never thought my romantic sister would settle for anything else. She found a Christmas romance and was able to keep the family together."

"That's fantastic. Jes is more amazing than I knew. So does that mean the girls aren't biologically hers?"

"No. Peg's eggs weren't healthy enough for the process. So Michael's sperm was used to fertilize Jes's eggs. Kari and Kami are their children. Jes would say it was meant to be."

"What happened with Peg?"

"She left, moved to Denver, and last I saw her she was engaged to another man. She decided she didn't want the children because they weren't hers biologically."

"How sad." She shook her head. "But it worked out for Jes and Michael in the end."

"Just like it will for us. I love you." He hugged her tight to him.

"You're too good for us but I love you."

They shared another brief kiss before he stepped back. "I'm going to change and give him a call." When she nodded he headed down the hallway toward the master bedroom where he could have privacy to fill Doctor Richard Bowmen in and he could change.

With each step his thoughts spun faster and faster. He wanted Richard's news to be positive, not just for the sake of having children with Ella, but also because the news she couldn't conceive could damage the progress he'd made with her. He didn't want her to close herself off from him, but more importantly, he didn't want to lose her back to that cabin in the woods again.

Chapter Fifteen

"You want to do what?" James couldn't believe what his sister was suggesting. Normally he'd do whatever he could to please her, but this might have been asking too much, especially right now. With Ella and Abbi living here he wasn't sure how they'd handle a bunch of people tramping through.

"It only makes sense to have the party here. I'm not going to have a new refrigerator until Monday. How am I going to keep the food cold, drinks, and what about the leftovers? Your house is big enough. Betty and I can handle everything, plus I have the catering staff coming. Please say yes, James, if not I'll have to cancel the Halloween party."

"What about Ella and Abbi? I don't know if they're ready for something like this. It's one thing to have it somewhere else where we can leave if it gets to be too much. But having it here, not to mention the preparations, we have less than twenty-four hours. There's no way we can get it all done."

"Sure we can." Ella stepped into the kitchen.

"What?" James turned to look at her. "You don't even know what she's asking."

"I heard what Jes is asking, and we can do it. Abbi is looking forward to the party, and you know what? So am I. Let's do this."

"Thank you so much." Jes hopped off the barstool she was sitting on and wrapped her arms around Ella. "This party is going to be a success thanks to you."

"This party wouldn't be happening if it wasn't for you." Michael smiled at Ella.

"Actually, it wouldn't be happening if it wasn't for either of them. This party was Jes's idea, she wanted to do something fun, and since it's not Christmas yet, she thought Halloween was the next best thing. Now, since Ella has committed my house as party central, well…you see where I'm going with this." James smirked at Michael. "Women."

"I'll make this up to you," Jes told him before turning her attention back to Ella. "He's such a downer, guess it's good I haven't told him that he's been roped into coming to the New Year's party."

"You've got to be kidding!" James looked from her to Michael. "Please tell me she isn't."

"Sorry, my friend, she is." Michael rubbed a hand over Jes's shoulders. "Maybe you two want to stay at Ella's tonight? Jes and I can have this place set up by morning, then the real fun begins."

"I don't mind helping," Ella offered, but Jessi shook her head.

"No, Michael's right. You've done enough, plus I want it to be a surprise for Abbi."

"Kicked out of my own home." James wrapped his arm around Ella's waist. "Come on, let's gather a few things and get on the road so Abbi can get to bed on time."

Ella nodded and let him lead her back to their bedroom. When they were out of hearing range, he whispered, "Did you find out anything?"

"You of all people know how this works. Doctors run test, they won't give complete answers until they've got all the results. He said he'd rush them as a favor to you, but we most likely won't know anything until next week sometime. How did you ever get me an appointment anyway?"

"We're colleagues and his office is right by mine. Oh, and I promised him a batch of Jessi's delicious brownies."

"Does she know?"

"Not yet but after having this party here she owes me big time."

She shook her head. "Go get your stuff, I'll let Abbi know and she can clean up her toys before we go."

"Such a good mother, always making her clean up." He leaned down and kissed her.

"She's never had so many toys, so who knows how much longer she'll be willing to clean up. I know when I was her age I fought my mother when she wanted me to put things away."

"Maybe we won't have that with her. She's responsible beyond her years and she listens like no other child I've seen. You're a remarkable parent."

On that note they parted ways as she went to Abbi's bedroom, and he continued into the one they shared. He was tempted to call Richard to see if there was anything he could tell from the exam before they headed to the cabin and away from cell reception, but knowing

Richard, if there was something to report he'd have already called. Now, they just had to wait and see. The waiting was always the hard part.

* * *

Ella opened the front door to James's house and was stunned. She couldn't believe the transformation in only a few hours. Halloween decorations everywhere, not including the front yard which had been made up to look like a graveyard.

"Hey, Ella. James with you?" Jessi stood on the ladder over the fireplace putting up a Halloween wreath.

"Yeah, Abbi's here too. What can we do?"

"Send James to help Michael, he's around back finishing the dresses."

"I heard and I'm going. I don't even want to know what the dresses are." James tossed his overnight back by the door and went out the door to make his way around the house.

"He might not want to know, but I do. So what are these dresses?" Ella asked, shutting the door behind them.

"It's chicken wire we cut into the shapes of dresses, then spray-painted with glow in the dark paint. Tonight they will light up and look like there are ghosts walking through our makeshift graveyard." Jessi adjusted the wreath a little to the right until it was perfect. "Michael completed the calls to the guests this morning and everyone knows to come here. The catering company will be here in a few hours with addition food."

"Well, what can I do?"

"Abbi." Jessi came to kneel before her. "My twins Kari and Kami are in the guest room next to yours with my housekeeper Betty. Would you like to go play with them?"

"Can I?" Abbi looked up at Ella.

"Go ahead, but remember they are just babies. Be careful with them, they're not like your dolls."

"She'll be fine. Betty's there," Jessi assured her. "Now you can help me with the last few items. Then we can get ready for the party. I hope you don't mind if we just change here. I've got a makeshift nursery set up in the guest room so the girls are close, and Laya, J.C.'s sister, is going to watch them during the party so Betty can supervise the staff and we can enjoy ourselves."

"It's hours before the party."

"Try dressing twins, your husband, and yourself on a deadline." Jessi laughed. "The girls won't be at the party much but you know what this town is like, they're going to want to see Kari and Kami. If Abbi wants to stay in there, she can. Laya's little sister Kelly will be in there too, she will be five next month."

"Oh, a perfect playmate for Abbi. That's wonderful. J.C. is the one with eight younger siblings right? He's engaged to Rebecca."

"Yeah, he found a place here to reclaim his life after he left the service and convinced his mother to move the rest of the family here."

"James has been filling me in. Will Jordan and Chloe be here tonight? Maybe Gioven?" She really had hoped Gioven would call but there hadn't been any word since their last visit. It had taken everything in her not to go back to Winterbloom to try to see him again.

"Jordan, Chloe, and Bianca will be here. Gioven? You mean that Marine who's staying in one of the cabins? I don't know him, so he wasn't actually invited, but I guess Jordan could bring him if he's up for it. Is he thinking about settling in Clearwater? We already have three former Marines, what's another one."

"I don't know if he's thinking of staying here." Ella shrugged, not wanting to go into more details or to explain how she had met him. "Let's get this done. I don't want you rushing around trying to get ready while the guests are arriving. I might have convinced James to have the party here, but I have no desire to play hostess."

"Well, for the New Year's party I'm hoping you'll co-hostess with me. It'll be fun."

Ella glanced out the window toward where the white tent had been set up. "At the end of December where do you plan to put everyone? It's not like you can do a tent like you have now with the bobbing for apples station and everything else. You're going to have to do it all inside."

"We'll have less activates. Plus, it's about the ball dropping, getting your midnight kiss, not about the fall games. It's going to be fun, and once winter sets in, the town residents don't see each other as much. There are no events at the lake, or picnics, so we live for things like this."

"I guess. The winter months get long, that's for sure. Let's see how this goes and then we can talk about the next party."

"I'm going to hold you to that."

Ella had no doubts Jessi would do just that but before she could say anything the phone rang. "I'll get it."

"If it's a cancellation tell them we won't hear of it and they'd better be here."

She just shook her head as she brought the phone to her ear. "Hello."

"Is this Ella Carmichael?" A male voice came through the line.

"Umm, yes." She tried not to panic. "Who's this?"

"Doctor Bowmen. I know you're getting ready for the party but I have some news from your appointment yesterday…that…you—"

"Hello? Are you still there?" She shook the phone like that would help. "Doctor Bowmen?"

"Everything okay?" Jessi popped her head from the refrigerator where she was grabbing the apples.

"I don't know what happened. He was there and now nothing." She stared down at the phone and refused to cry. *What news?*

"You said Doctor Bowmen? Was he cancelling?"

"No, he…" She wasn't sure what to say.

"Here." Jes took the phone from her and pushed some buttons before she brought it to her ear. "It's just going straight to voicemail. It's possible he's out of cell coverage."

"It's fine." She slammed her hand on the counter, terrified it was news she didn't want to hear. "I just need a minute." She took off down the hall toward the master bedroom before Jessi could say anything to stop her. She needed time to gather herself, to get her thoughts to settle before she could face anyone.

* * *

The last of the Halloween dresses was in place in the yard, while James and Michael took a moment to stand back and study their handy work. He'd thought the idea was bizarre to say the least, but it actually looked pretty good.

"James!" Jes came marching toward them.

"You'd have made a good drill instructor," he joked.

"You need to go inside."

"What's wrong? Is something wrong with Ella or Abbi?"

"Ella got a call from Doctor Bowmen and then she took off. The call got dropped. I tried him back but it just goes to voicemail. Is she pregnant or something?"

"No." He tossed the hammer on the ground. "Damn it, just give us a few minutes. Can you make sure Abbi's okay and stays away for a bit?"

"She's with the girls and Betty, but I'll make sure she stays there."

With that he took off to the house in a steady jog. With each step, he slowed his pace until he was in the hallway to the bedrooms.

He slipped past without anyone noticing and made it to the bedroom. "Ella?" He pushed the slightly ajar door open, and when he didn't see her he called out again. "Sweetie?"

"I'm here." A hand waved at him from the other side of the bed. She was crying.

He went around the bed to find her sitting on the floor, her legs pulled tight against her chest. "Oh, Ella, come here." He sank down next to her and pulled her against him. "It's going to be okay."

"You don't know that. He could have called to tell me I'll never be able to have kids." She sobbed. "Wait, how do you know?"

"Jessi found me and told me you received a call from Richard but it was dropped. Cell phone service can be spotty around here, you know that. Especially in the winter or during a storm."

"It's not storming." She tried to reason between tears.

"The wind is picking up out there, so you don't know what it's like on the mountains. Richard lives on the edge of town, on the mountain." He ran his hand up and down her arm, soothing her. "It's going to be okay. Richard will be here soon and he'll tell you whatever he knows. Whatever it is, we'll get through it *together*."

He wasn't sure how much time had passed as he sat there, comforting her, telling her things would work out, when there was a knock at the door.

"Not now." He growled at whoever disturbed them.

"James." Jes pushed the door opened a little.

"Not now, Jes. Whatever it is can wait."

"Richard is here. He's asking to speak with both of you. I figured you wanted privacy so I asked him to wait in your home office. Will you see him or do you want me to ask him to come back?"

"We'll see him." Ella wiped the tears away. "Tell him we'll be right there. Thanks, Jes."

"You're welcome." She closed the door.

"Are you sure? I can talk to him first if you'd like."

"No, just give me a moment." She slipped into the bathroom to take care of her makeup, which had run with her tears.

Suddenly uneasy, he tried to reassure himself that Richard wouldn't drop bad news on them before the party. That whatever he'd found out had to be hopeful, or he would have waited until Monday to deliver the news out of professional courtesy.

One thing after another seemed to hit them, and he just hoped Richard's news wasn't going to be another blow. He wasn't sure how many more Ella could handle. Not having children with her would be a disappointment, but he refused to allow it to keep them apart. The love they shared was too strong to let this break them.

* * *

Ella took the seat James offered, wrenching her hands as nervousness made her stomach roil. Part of her wanted to demand what the test showed while the other part told her it was news she really didn't want to know. That if she didn't ask, he wouldn't tell her, and she could go on without knowing how much she'd screwed up her body.

"Ms. Carmichael," Doctor Bowmen began.

"Call me Ella, please."

James laid his hand on her shoulder. "Richard, I know you can be long-winded so just cut to it. What did you find out?"

"I told you when you gave birth to Abbi that due to the complications it could make having more children impossible."

"I know," she snapped. "I'm sorry. I just need to know if I screwed up. I wanted to give Abbi siblings, but until I met James I didn't think it would be possible." She reached up and laid her hand over his.

"As I said I rushed the tests and when I was at the hospital checking on another patient I received the results. I was on my way back to my place to get ready for the party, when the cell service dropped our call. When I couldn't get through I turned around because I knew you'd want to know." He paused and smiled. "Ella, everything is fine with you. You can have more children. Though if you're going to begin trying, I suggest you start a prenatal vitamin to get some of the levels that are borderline low a little higher."

"I can have children," she repeated, trying to swallow the news as tears rolled down her face.

"Yes, I don't see any reason why you shouldn't have a healthy pregnancy. Some of the issues you encountered at the end were due to your lack of prenatal care. I suspect it won't happen next time." Richard glanced up at James.

"No, she'll receive regular prenatal visits." He squeezed her shoulder. "See, sweetie, I told you everything would be fine."

"Oh, thank you, Doctor Bowmen. I can't tell you how much this means to me."

"Richard, please, and I'm glad I could bring you good news. I'll drop the prenatal vitamins in James's office for you on Monday. Now I better get home and get ready for this party. I'll see you later."

"I'll see you out," James offered.

"There's no need. I can find my way and I think you two could use a minute." Richard smirked. "Congratulations."

"I can't believe it," she whispered as the door shut.

He took her hands and pulled her to her feet. "I told you everything would work out. We can give Abbi siblings, as many as you want. Which reminds me, I spoke to the construction foreman while I was outside. He was driving past and saw me decorating."

"The house…" Part of her expected the news they wouldn't be able to break ground until spring, but she refused to let that deflate her mood.

"They broke ground this past week. With the double crew I hired and the promise of a good Christmas bonus if they finished by the deadline, I'm making this happen."

"Deadline?" She raised an eyebrow at him.

"We'll be in the house by Christmas and we can give Abbi a proper Christmas in our new house."

"Are you serious?"

"Yes. The bonus, some strings pulled with Michael's help, and I managed it. Construction crews don't have as much work around here, especially this time of the year, so they were happy to do it."

She wiped the palms of her hands on her jeans. "There's one more thing I'd like to do before the holidays."

"What's that, sweetie? You name it and I'll make it happen."

"Is that marriage proposal still on the table?"

He took a step back and tipped his head at her like he was trying to figure out if she was serious. "It will never be taken off the table until I have you as my wife. That and I want to adopt Abbi so she has our name."

"Can you make it happen before Christmas? I want to be Mrs. Macis before we move into our house."

"Do you want the Father to marry us? Dale said you were raised Catholic."

"No, I mean…unless you want him. I'd rather just the judge. I was raised that way, but I'm not raising Abbi Catholic. I'm teaching her about many different religions, so one day when she's old enough she can choose if she wants to practice any of them, or if she wants to pull from different ones to create her own beliefs."

"A judge is fine with me. I'll speak with him tonight about it."

"There's one more thing. I want to get married at the place we met, the cabin. I know it's not fancy but I want our vows done there, then we can go wherever for the reception because I know once Jes hears she's not going to let me off the hook without one, it's another excuse for a party."

He closed the distance between them. "I love you, and I can't wait to have you as my wife."

"I love you too."

Small Town Doctor

Epilogue

The wedding reception was in full swing and all Ella wanted to do was slip away with her new husband for some alone time. She still couldn't believe she was married but James was the man she'd always dreamed about when she pictured herself married. It was unbelievable they'd managed to throw a wedding together in only two weeks. That way they could spend Thanksgiving and the rest of the holiday season as an official married couple.

"How's my wife?" James came up beside her.

"Unbelievably happy. Look at those two, they are living it up." She nodded to where Abbi and Kelly danced in the middle of the dance floor. The two girls had quickly become friends. Through the crowd, she caught a glimpse of her parents chatting with some of their friends. They couldn't have been happier for Ella. "Where were you?"

"Lawrence Meyers." He held up a white envelope. "Adoption papers. I'm now officially Abbi's father."

"No, you're her dad. A father can be someone who's just there, but a dad is someone who reads bedtime stories, plays with dolls because it makes his little girl happy. That's you. She loves you."

"I love her too. She's the greatest little girl a dad could ask for."

"Good thing I told her *yes* when she asked me earlier if she could call you Daddy." She slipped her arm around his waist. "Hope you don't mind."

"Not at all."

"Excuse me," a voice called from behind them.

She turned to find Gioven standing there in his tux, looking slightly uncomfortable. "Gioven."

"I can tell you're surprised to see me."

"I am. I sent the invite to Jordan and Chloe, mentioning you as well, but I didn't think you'd come." She reached out but stopped before she touched his arm. "It's good to see you."

"I wanted to come to apologize. When you came by Winterbloom I was an ass, I'm sorry for that. I haven't had a drink in two weeks."

"That's wonderful." She gave him one of the biggest smiles she could.

"It didn't feel very good, but now that I'm sober I can see things a little better. I've got to go back to Virginia to tend to a few things but I'm going to stay here through the holidays and then I'll see. Maybe Clearwater isn't too bad after all and I can settle down here like all my comrades. I'm sure I can find somewhere to put my skills to use."

"Jordan mentioned you're handy with a hammer. I have a double construction team working on our house. If they're still working when you get back, maybe you want to join them. The extra hands would be beneficial considering the deadline is two weeks before Christmas. We want to be moved in so we can give Abbi a proper Christmas in our new home." James shrugged. "It's an offer, a standing one at that. So you can take it or leave it."

"I appreciate it. I didn't want to miss this but I'm leaving in the morning. I should be back in a few days and I'll be in touch." Gioven turned his attention back to her and laid his hand on her arm. "You look beautiful, and thank you for everything." With that, he walked away, back toward the table where Jordan, the other former Marines, and their wives sat.

"I'd say things are going to work out for Gioven." James kissed her temple.

"I hope so." She leaned into his embrace. "Now, can we slip out of here and enjoy our one night together before Abbi rejoins us?"

He glanced toward Abbi. "She's going to be fine. A sleepover with Kelly at Jes and Michael's. She's in safe hands. Stop worrying."

"Parents never stop worrying." She watched her daughter learn the hokey-pokey. "I've never spent a night away from her."

"We're only going to be right down the road and I promise your mind will be on other things."

"What if she gets sick or something in the middle of the night?"

He chuckled. "She's staying with a pediatrician, I think Michael can handle his niece if anything comes up and you know Jes will call. Now let's say our goodbyes because I want you all to myself. Maybe we can start trying for a sibling for Abbi."

She laced her fingers between his and nodded. Everything he said was true and she knew it. There was just an underlying fear being away from her daughter, especially for the first time. This was the life she wanted, now she needed to enjoy it. Life would be what she made it, and when she took her vows as his wife, she made a silent vow to make it the best she could. "I love you."

"As I love you, Mrs. Macis."

Marissa Dobson

Born and raised in the Pittsburgh, Pennsylvania area, Marissa Dobson now resides about an hour from Washington, D.C. She's a lady who likes to keep busy, and is always busy doing something. With two different college degrees, she believes you're never done learning.

Being the first daughter to an avid reader, this gave her the advantage of learning to read at a young age. Since learning to read she has always had her nose in a book. It wasn't until she was a teenager that she started writing down the stories she came up with.

Marissa is blessed with a wonderful supportive husband, Thomas. He's her other half and allows her to stay home and pursue her writing. He puts up with all her quirks and listens to her brainstorm in the middle of the night.

Her writing buddies Max (a cocker spaniel) and Dawne (a beagle mix) are always around to listen to her bounce ideas off them. They might not be able to answer, but they are helpful in their own ways.

She love to hear from readers so send her an email at marissa@marissadobson.com or visit her online at http://www.marissadobson.com.

Small Town Doctor

Other Books by Marissa Dobson

Alaskan Tigers:

Tiger Time

The Tiger's Heart

Tigress for Two

Night with a Tiger

Trusting a Tiger

Jinx's Mate

Two for Protection

Bearing Secrets

Stormkin:

Storm Queen

Reaper:

A Touch of Death

Beyond Monogamy:

Theirs to Tresure

Small Town Doctor

SEALed for You:

Ace in the Hole

Explosive Passion

Capturing a Diamond

Operation Family

Cedar Grove Medical:

Hope's Toy Chest

Destiny's Wish

Fate Series:

Snowy Fate

Sarah's Fate

Mason's Fate

As Fate Would Have It

Half Moon Harbor Resort:

Learning to Live

Learning What Love Is

Her Cowboy's Heart

Half Moon Harbor Resort Volume One

Clearwater:

Winterbloom

Unexpected Forever

Losing to Win

www.ingramcontent.com/pod-product-compliance
Lightning Source LLC
Chambersburg PA
CBHW022118170626
46808CB00002B/760